A

Bantam Books

A MALI ANDERSON MYSTERY

TOAST BEFORE DYING

"TENSE AND
EXPERTLY
CRAFTED."
—*Chicago Tribune*

GRACE F. EDWARDS

AUTHOR OF *IF I SHOULD DIE*

DON'T MISS THE FIRST
MALI ANDERSON MYSTERY
BY GRACE F. EDWARDS

IF I SHOULD DIE

> "THE BEST CRIME FICTION
> ABOUT HARLEM SINCE
> CHESTER HIMES."
> —Eleanor Taylor Bland

AVAILABLE WHEREVER
BANTAM BOOKS ARE SOLD

BANTAM BOOKS

ISBN 0-553-57953-3

US $5.99 / $8.99 CAN

9 780553 579536

50599

S

Also by Grace F. Edwards

In the Shadow of the Peacock
If I Should Die

a toast before dying

A MALI ANDERSON MYSTERY

grace f. edwards

BANTAM BOOKS
NEW YORK TORONTO
LONDON SYDNEY
AUCKLAND

This edition contains the complete text of the original hardcover edition.
NOT ONE WORD HAS BEEN OMITTED.

A TOAST BEFORE DYING

A Bantam Book / Published by arrangement with Doubleday,
a division of Random House, Inc.

PUBLISHING HISTORY
Doubleday hardcover edition published May 1998
Bantam paperback edition / March 1999

ISBN: 0-553-57953-3

Published simultaneously in the United States and Canada

Bantam Books are published by Bantam Books, a division of Random House,
Inc. Its trademark, consisting of the words "Bantam Books" and the
portrayal of a rooster, is Registered in U.S. Patent and Trademark Office and
in other countries. Marca Registrada. Bantam Books, 1540 Broadway, New
York, New York 10036.

PRINTED IN THE UNITED STATES OF AMERICA

WCD   10 9 8 7 6 5 4 3 2

Dedicated to my daughter Perri A. Edwards,
and to my granddaughter Simone

acknowledgments

My thanks to the members of the Harlem Writers Guild, Inc., especially Bill Banks, Donis Ford, and Sarah Elizabeth Wright for their unwavering love and support.

chapter one

I leaned hard on the bell next door to Bertha's Beauty Shop as Ruffin paced nervously beside me. It was 4 A.M. and except for a solitary figure half a block away who slipped into the shadow of an abandoned building, Eighth Avenue was deserted.

Even the twenty-four-hour bodega across the street that dispensed milk, soda, beer, and cigarettes through the narrow slot in its iron shutter had turned off the multicolored strobe light.

One block north, a patrol car turned into 135th Street heading for the precinct. I could hear the thrum of the car's motor in the quiet.

. . . Where is Bertha? She had phoned in the middle of the night, crying. Where is she?

Through the window of the shop, I made out the circular stairway in the rear that led up to her apartment. The night-light was on but I could see no one.

Ruffin crouched low on the cool pavement, wagging his tail, watching as I reached into my pocket for a quarter, snaked my hand through the metal grill, and rapped on the window. The echo sounded as if glass were breaking.

I withdrew my hand and thought again about what brought me here. Bertha had been crying, trying to tell me something about Kendrick. There had been noise and we'd gotten disconnected.

I leaned against the metal shutter and glanced up and down the deserted avenue, trying to keep my thoughts from racing. Maybe she was at the precinct, at Harlem Hospital's emergency room. Or at the morgue.

Suddenly Ruffin rose to his feet and let out a short growl, low and deep.

"Ruffin! What's the matter?"

He pressed on the leash and I had to pull back hard to restrain him. He didn't exactly relax, but there was less resistance and I eased up. If he wanted to, he could have taken off and dragged me for half a block. But he was a well-trained Great Dane.

Still, I held the leash and reined him in tightly when Flyin' Home rolled up in his wheelchair, being pulled along by his two German shepherds. The dogs were large and reminded me of St. Nick's reindeers, except they were not in the business of delivering Christmas gifts. They spotted Ruffin and were ready for battle. The barking could be heard for blocks.

"Yo! Shut the fuck *up*!" Flyin' Home yelled. "Can't take you asses nowhere 'thout y'all actin' up."

Flyin' Home was twenty-eight years old, with powerful brown arms and the deceptively round face of an angel. Up until three years ago, when he'd had the use of his legs, he'd been known as the Artist—as in escape artist (specifically, fire escapes). He'd been known to scale them up, down, and sideways; pop a window gate, and scoop an assortment of what he called "alphabet appliances"—PCs, TVs, and VCRs. And he usually made it back down to the street in the time it took the snoring victim to turn over.

He had worked unarmed, and one night he'd come through the window of an insomniac propped in bed cradling a Mossberg pump shotgun with a twenty-inch-long barrel.

The blast had taken care of the Artist's lower spine and had left him navigating in a chair ever since. The chair was motorized, but as his legs had grown smaller he'd gotten the dogs because, he said, they moved faster. He traveled at top speed and his girlfriend had stenciled the name Flyin' Home on the back of the chair.

I waited as he spoke to the dogs again. Then in the sudden silence he nodded to me, but his eyes were scanning the avenue.

"You lookin' for Bert? She at the Half-Moon. Somebody got capped."

"What? Who? Who was it?"

"I 'ont know and I 'ont care," he said quickly, still looking around. "Blueshirts on the scene, bad for my health." He gave the slightest snap of the leather harnesses and the dogs rose at once.

"Flyin', wait! Who was there? Did you see anything?"

"Hell, no. And you ain't on the force no more, so why you wanna know?"

"I'm not on the force, but you and I go back a long way."

"I'm cool with that, Mali. And since we go back, you oughtta know my motto: When shit go down, I leaves town."

With that, he clicked his teeth and the chair took off, rumbling quickly over the pavement. It picked up speed, and in a blink Flyin' Home was a block away.

I watched as he disappeared down Eighth Avenue. . . . Somebody got capped. Shot. And Bert had screamed on the phone, "They got Kendrick, Mali! They got my brother!"

Huge spotlights cast a blue-white glow over the Half-Moon Bar, and the entire corner of 140th Street and Seventh Avenue was cordoned off as if a major film crew had set up operations. The crowd pressing against the barricades was larger than at most parades, and I understood why Eighth Avenue was so deserted. Everyone had run to where the action was.

I couldn't maneuver into the crowd with Ruffin, so I skirted the periphery. "What happened?"

A man and a woman glanced at me, then at Ruffin, and backed away. "I don't know. Somebody got killed, is all we know."

I kept moving, asking, until someone, a slim teenager seated safely out of reach atop a parked car, looked down at me and nodded. "Barmaid. They just took her from the alley."

An older woman standing on the other side of the car chimed in. "Today was her birthday. Big sign in the window all week. Somebody said she had just had a birthday toast. Then she got blown away. Ain't that somethin'? Don't know from one day to the next what's in store for you."

I stood there for a moment, allowing the news to sink in. It was not Kendrick who'd been killed, but Thea. It was Thea, the most popular barmaid in Harlem.

The milling crowd was so thick I couldn't see beyond the outer edges. Some of the uniformed officers that I recognized on the scene would not have offered me much in the way of information, and Tad Honeywell was not there. I would've spotted him. I moved away. Kendrick had not been killed, but Bertha had said, "They got my brother." Where was he? And where was she? I circled the crowd again, hoping to catch sight of them.

An hour later, only one crime-scene van remained, and the crowd began to thin out. At 5 A.M. I left also, turning into 139th Street toward home.

The phone was ringing and I knew it was Bertha before I picked it up. Her voice sounded old.

"Listen, I'm home. Can you stop by later?"

"I heard what happened, Bertha. I'll see you in a few minutes."

Dad hadn't gotten in from his gig at the Club Harlem so I propped a note on the piano and left the house again. Dawn was a weak glow pushing against the gray sky and the chatter of busy birds kept me company all the way to Eighth Avenue.

Bertha's Beauty Shop was two blocks away, situated between a small Laundromat and a store that sold balloons and party favors. Bertha's shutter was now rolled up.

When she opened the door, tears welled up even before she spoke. "Come on in. You don't know what I been through. You don't know . . ."

"What happened? Thea's dead. How did it happen?"

I followed her inside. The front of the shop was in semidarkness and the cool air had not yet been sucked out into the July heat by the steady opening and closing of the door. Bertha had come downstairs from her apartment wearing a pink silk dress edged in rhinestones. She apparently had not had time to change. The dress was torn and dirty, her hair was a mass of auburn tangles, and her face was puffed from crying.

"Listen," I said, "go get yourself together while I fix some coffee. Laura's Luncheonette is probably open by now. I'll run out for some breakfast."

Without a word, she disappeared up the stairs again. I plugged in the coffeemaker, and by the time I returned, the coffee was perking, and Bertha was sitting in the chair by the window in her usual jeans and T-shirt. I handed her a plate of grits, eggs, and bacon.

"So, you heard . . . ?"

"Not everything. I still don't know what happened."

"That's what everybody in the Half-Moon was askin'. 'What happened?' Well, Thea was shot dead in that alley back of the bar. Kendrick's in jail. Henderson Laws, that son of a bitch, heard the shot and come runnin' out the door sayin' my brother did it, that Kendrick had shot her. I was there. I know he didn't do it. But the cops took Henderson Laws's word, and now my brother's in jail."

She put down her fork and leaned back in her chair. She closed her eyes and I was amazed at how drawn her face looked even though she was only thirty-six, just four years older than me.

Kendrick was twenty-six years old and so good-looking that given half the chance he would put Denzel in the shade. He made you want to holler when he parted that fine mouth to smile at you.

Henderson Laws owned the Half-Moon, and Thea and Kendrick had worked behind the bar.

"You say you were there. Did you see what happened?"

"Well, I mean . . . I kinda saw it and didn't see it."

I looked at her. "What does that mean?"

She moved from the chair and toward the counter where the brushes, scissors, hair oils, shampoos, creams, and color charts lay. It was still early, barely 7 A.M., but from habit she plugged in the outlet connecting the rack of iron straightening combs. Then she picked up a towel and pointed to an empty chair.

"Listen, I know you don't need it, short as your hair is, but how about a conditioner. I can talk better when my hands are workin'."

I shrugged and sat in the chair and she fastened the plastic cape around my shoulder. She applied an egg-and-mayonnaise mixture that felt cold but soon warmed up as her fingers massaged my scalp.

"So start at the beginning. You never go to that bar. How come you were there last night? And what happened to your dress?"

"Well, you know—" Bertha stopped talking when the brass bell over the door jingled and two women came in together. Mid-thirties and well dressed. I had never seen them before and neither had Bertha, judging from her expression. Neither one had an appointment. I glanced at the clock over the mirror.

Seven-fifteen, especially on a Saturday, wasn't too early for a "walk-in," as the beauticians called them. Most small operators—unlike the major salons—usually accommodated walk-ins, hoping they'd return if they were satisfied with the work.

These women seemed anxious, and after a minute or so I wondered if they were here to find out about Kendrick. Or had they been in the bar, part of the night crowd who decided to drop in for the real deal to take back to their friends.

The taller woman had medium-brown skin with longish hair pulled back in a ponytail held by a wide barrette. The other woman was dark and pretty with wide eyes under a close feathered haircut.

Bertha did not hesitate: "Good morning. What

can I do for you?" She placed a plastic cap on my head, not at all gently, and the mirror reflected her annoyance. She was civil but her straight face let them know that today she wasn't ready to handle anything except dead presidents—as many Jacksons as possible and preferably a few Grants.

The two women glanced at each other and it became clear that they were not together. They had simply walked in the door at the same time. The ponytail, the taller of the two, spoke first and wasted no words.

"I want to know why your brother killed Thea."

The silence lasted longer than I expected. It was broken by Bertha's tight whisper. "What did you . . . say?"

"You heard me. I want to know—" Before the woman got the rest of the words out, Bertha was down from the stool, scooping up a blazing straightening comb from the rack.

"Raise up, bitch! My brother didn't kill nobody!"

Bertha was less than five feet three and Miss Ponytail was as tall as I am, five nine. But what Bertha might have lacked in height she made up for in volume.

"You gonna eat them words or eat this heat!"

The other woman, the feather-cut, seemed horrified and backed toward the door but did not open it.

"Wait! Wait a minute," I said, stepping in front of Bertha to face the woman. "Who are you? What do you mean coming in here with a question like that?"

The woman looked at me as if seeing me for the first time.

"I have a right. Thea . . . was my friend."

Her eyes were wide with anger and I could see the tears threatening to spill over.

"Look, you're upset. Why don't you sit down. Then we can talk. We can—"

"Aw no!" Bertha said, pushing me aside. "Bitch come in with attitude and you makin' her at home? Fuck her. Let her get her ass on out my door. Right now!"

"Bert, please. Wait a minute. Let me—"

"Let you nuthin'! Whose side you on anyway?"

A red tinge had spread across her brown face, and I knew the last thing she needed was a stroke.

"Okay. Okay. She's leaving."

I intended to walk outside with the woman, get a phone number, and contact her later. Any information she had might help, but right now Bertha was too angry to see it.

"So what you waitin' for, bitch? Get the fuck on out!"

"Don't you dare speak to me like that!"

"I'll dare the devil if he come on wrong. Now don't you like it, don't you take it. Here's my shoulder, come on shake it!"

I stepped out of the way. Scars have a habit of staying with me, so I wasn't about to connect with Bertha's hot comb. The decibel level was so high that no one heard the bell jingle.

Framed in the doorway was a third woman and we all turned to stare.

"Pardon me. Which one of you is Kendrick's sister?"

The four of us already crowded in the small space now looked at this new person. Clearly she had not come to have her hair done. Even under the deep crown of her straw hat, we could see the pale blond strands pushed to the side. Her thin shoulders were held back as if by a brace and she carried a large straw bag loosely in the crook of her arm. Her blue eyes took in the scene and she seemed undecided about stepping any farther into the shop.

"Who are you?" I asked.

She hesitated for a fraction of a second, long enough for me to know a lie was coming.

"I'm . . . Teddi Lovette. His agent."

She tried to smile but her voice shook.

"Come in," I said, even though I knew she was lying.

Bert still had not shifted gears sufficiently to open her mouth without screaming, and Miss Ponytail used the moment to head out.

"Well, okay," I said to no one in particular and followed like a hostess seeing a guest to the door.

Once outside, I caught Miss Ponytail's arm.

"Just a minute. I want to apologize. Bert's upset."

"So am I," the woman said and continued to walk. My legs are long but the woman moved so fast I had a problem keeping up. I trotted beside her, feeling the egg-and-mayo mixture beginning to ooze down my neck from under the cap.

"Listen, I knew Thea also. She was a sweet person and what happened to her was terrible. An awful thing."

We reached the corner and the light changed.

"I know you're too upset to talk right now, but could I call you?"

She fumbled in her purse. When she finally extended her card, I snatched it before the light changed again.

"How well did you know Thea?" she asked.

I stood there, praying for the light to change once more and struggling for an answer that would sound at least half-truthful.

She nodded her head. "Because you must be mistaken. Thea . . . was not a sweet person."

Then she stepped off the curb, crossed Eighth Avenue, and opened the door to a silver Lexus. I rushed back to the shop but when I entered, Bert's hot comb was resting in the rack and Blondie and the dark pretty woman had both disappeared.

chapter two

I looked around, half-expecting to find them hiding behind the coatrack.

"What happened?"

"Nuthin,' " Bert said, extending a card. "This is from Blondie. She asked me about Thea. Wants me to call her when I feel up to talkin'. Then she left. The other one musta been scared to death 'cause she backed out before this one did. Moved like somebody was chasin' her. Don't know who she was."

"Damn." I sat down as Bert walked to the sink and filled the small coffeepot again. This was going to be a three-pot day plus aspirin. I studied the card: "Teddi Lovette. Voice Technique and Acting Coach."

"I thought she said she was his agent?"

"Well, who knows what the hell she is." Bert shrugged. "Probably like Hallmark and got a card for every occasion. I knew she was bogus when she stepped in. Sure is a surprise though. I didn't know my brother was dippin' his biscuit in cream."

"There you go jumping to conclusions. We don't know what the connection is."

"You right, Mali. I should'na said that. Least till you can call and get the real deal."

I looked at her. "Me? You want me to call?"

"Well, you bein' an ex-cop 'n' all, I figured you'd know the kinda stuff to ask."

I did not answer. Ex-cop. I'm an ordinary citizen now with a three-year-old lawsuit pending against the NYPD for being fired.

I sat in the chair and took the plastic cap off my head. The egg-and-mayo combo had congealed into meringue-like peaks and I wondered if I had any hair left under there. Bert saw my expression.

"Don't worry. That ain't no chemical job you lookin' at. That's all natural."

So is nightshade, I wanted to say, but Bert was in no mood for back talk.

"Let's get it washed out and I can finish tellin' you. See, I don't know what got me outta the house last night. Maybe it's this damn July heat and my AC ain't kickin' too tough. Maybe I was tired of sleazebag Geraldo gettin' off on O.J. And tired of listenin' to Jenny Jones and the same old stupid shit about whose white mama done stole which daughter's damn dumb black boyfriend. I mean, where do they get those fools from?"

Her voice sounded as if she'd been running and could not catch her breath. I nodded and leaned back in the chair. She rinsed my hair and lathered on something else.

"So I got dressed and went out. 'Cause you know the bar's not that far away. And Kendrick had sounded so angry when he called, like he had just got some more bad news or somethin'. I figured I'd sit with him till maybe he cooled down some."

"Angry about what?" I asked.

I knew Kendrick was working hard to break into acting and tended bar at the Half-Moon between bit parts, fashion shows, and casting calls. He had recently signed a major modeling contract and was about to do a show in Milan.

"I didn't know he had time to feel angry," I said.

"C'mon, Mali, you know that every good-bye ain't gone even though he and Thea broke up a couple of months ago. He was still upset about it and they'd had words earlier in the bar. That's why he called me. To talk.

"I knew she wasn't right for him, but what could I say? Imagine tellin' somebody that you tired of 'im. That's what she said. Not 'I don't love you no more' or 'I met somebody else' but 'I'm tired of you.' Just like that. I knew that girl from way back and peeped her card from the jump.

"From a long time ago, when she first started enterin' them beauty contests, she was stuck on herself. First it was her wigs, then the weaves—girl bought more hair than Diana Ross. And you know Thea sure didn't need all that. She already had fine soft hair— what we used to call 'good stuff' back in the day. But she wanted her strands even straighter. And the straighter it got, the madder she got, for some reason . . . till finally I had to tell her I wasn't puttin' no more heat to her scalp. I mean I need a dollar but I got my ethics."

"Not to mention your insurance premiums," I reminded her.

"That too. Then one day, she up and cut her hair as short as yours and didn't need me no more. But I decided to stay friends with her 'cause by then Kendrick's nose was wide open. She had him eatin' outta her hand and I meant to see that the fool didn't choke."

I nodded. Kendrick stopped by every day. When I was here, I was especially glad to see him, because two years ago, as busy as he was, he had taken time out to help me with my nephew, Alvin. Knicks games, fishing trips, movies, in-line skating in Central Park, swimming at the Y. Things that helped the boy cope with the death of his mother and father.

Kendrick had stepped in and now was like part of my family and I loved him. Thank God Alvin was in St. Croix and not here to see this mess. But he'd be back in August. I wondered what I could do before he returned.

I looked around the shop as Bertha removed the towel. Of course I didn't need to visit a salon to have my two inches of hair taken care of, but the deep conditioner and the scalp and neck massage were what kept me coming here. That and my long friendship with Miss Bertha.

I grew up not too far from the shop—on Strivers Row. Miss Bert—I call her that sometimes even though there's not much difference in our ages—grew up uptown near the Polo Ground Houses where her daddy's two-chair barbershop fronted his numbers enterprise.

Years ago he had hit big and gave his daughter five thousand dollars the day she finished the Poro School of Beauty Culture. "Buy that Cadillac you wanted," he'd said.

Instead she'd bought an empty, rundown two-story building on Frederick Douglass Boulevard and transformed it into a cozy beauty shop with two rental apartments upstairs, one in which she now lived.

I had met her when I was eighteen and my father had finally persuaded me to impose some order on my wild, thick hairstyle. I'd been coming here so long that now I usually strolled in without an appointment, sometimes just to sit and listen to the latest talk—who hit a number, who died, and who black folks oughtta vote for the next time around.

It was a two-operator shop, and since the other beautician had left to open her own place, Bertha worked alone.

I sat in the chair, listening to Bertha and wanting to see Kendrick poke his handsome face in the door and wave to me, but that wasn't going to happen. What in the world was I going to tell Alvin when I called him?

"I don't know how it all happened," she continued. "And so quick. I was right there. I heard the shot. Seen that flash from the gun. Now Thea's gone and my brother's in jail. I still can't believe this."

The few times I had stopped in the bar, Thea had not been there, but I had seen her here, in this very chair. She was tall and thin with deep-set eyes and skin the color of pale parchment. She was also a singer and Dad had once said that her figure reminded him of a taller version of Vanessa Williams but that her voice had an unalterably sad quality—like an old-time blues singer at an after-hours session nursing a glass of Scotch.

Thea had had several gigs at the Club Harlem with Dad's jazz quartet and she had been pretty popular. She had been popular in the Half-Moon also, yet when she stepped out in the middle of the night someone had been waiting.

Bertha's usually steady hands were shaking, and I was glad I wasn't having my hair straightened. Considering how distracted she was, I was grateful I was only getting a deep conditioner.

"What happened when you got to the bar, before Thea got shot?" I asked.

"Well"—she settled on the high stool and reached for a second cup of coffee—"Kendrick also said there was a party goin' on. Thea's birthday. Wall-to-wall men. That kinda stuff. He think I'm lookin' for a husband again and I should check out the scene. I keep tellin' him one bad round was enough, but he don't believe me. Think a woman ain't complete without somethin' warmin' her in the winter and coolin' her in the summer. Right now, I try to be cool all by myself, 'cause the last friend I had said he was steppin' out for some Trojans and musta gone to a store in Australia 'cause that was Christmas Eve and I ain't even got a postcard.

"Anyway, the place was crowded but I got a seat at the end of the bar. Whatever had gone down between Kendrick and Thea musta been heavy 'cause he looked like he was still mad even though he was smilin' for the crowd. But I could tell he was upset.

"Place was so busy Kendrick didn't have time for more than three words to me. And that politician Edwin Michaels was there. I guess he's makin' the rounds now that it's election time. People comin' up shakin' his hand like he was a king or somethin'. Man been in office twelve years and I ain't seen shit he done except maybe hop a plane to the islands every other month."

I knew Edwin Michaels vaguely. I had met him when my neighbor Dr. Thomas had hosted a fundraiser for him three years ago and again when he had dropped into the Club Harlem to hear Dad play. He imagined himself irresistible, and unfortunately some women, seduced by the aphrodisiac of power, reinforced the idea.

"Like I said, the place was jammed. I looked around and it seemed like everybody was stargazin' at themselves in the mirror over the bar as if the only person they wanted to meet was that one in the mirror.

"I didn't bother to waste my time 'cause this wasn't hardly my show. I got up to leave and waved to Kendrick as he came from behind the bar. Said he was goin' to get towels or somethin'. Then I waved to Thea. She had champagne in her hand, raisin' it in a toast, when the wall phone behind her rang. She picked it up and put down her glass real quick. Her face changed, like the call had surprised her. The volume was pumped so I couldn't hear what she said, but it couldn't have been more than two words. She hung up and slipped from behind the bar, movin' like she was Pryor on fire. I shoulda kept a tag on Kendrick. Things woulda been different if I had . . .

"I came out through that side door, the one lets you out on 140th Street instead of Seventh Avenue. That alleyway there should've had a light. It usually does but it was out. I wasn't scared 'cause it ain't but a hop and skip to the sidewalk. The streetlight was also out and I remember steppin' in somethin' and couldn't see exactly what. I was hopin' it was water and not somethin' some damn dog had left.

"Well, out the side of my eye as I'm bendin' down, I see somethin' move and realize somebody was there in front of me in the dark. No more than two feet away.

"I hear Thea's voice, soundin' kinda surprised. Maybe happy, even. I don't know. She made a little sound—like she was short of breath—then she said: 'It's you! Oh, it's you!'

"And that gun went off, not more than two inches from her nose. Me and Kendrick got to her at the same time. I don't know where he came from. I heard footsteps. But not runnin' footsteps. Somewhere in front of me.

"Next thing I know, he on his knees, yellin', 'I

didn't mean it! I didn't mean it!' and holdin' what was left of her head in his hands.

"I took one look and ran to the curb and everything in my stomach came up. By that time, the bar had emptied out into that alley. Couldn't even move. Henderson Laws was screamin' and grabbed Kendrick and started punchin' him. I ran back and started swingin' at Laws. I mean we got into it, I tried my best to snatch that dusty toupee, but he musta had that number cemented on. Somebody separated us but I got in some good licks. Never did like that man. And when the cops come, Laws right away said he heard Kendrick say he had did it, had killed her."

She paused and in the silence we listened to the early rush of Eighth Avenue traffic. The air still held that slight damp coolness but by noontime the July sun would be on us and the baking asphalt would be throwing the heat back at anyone on the street.

Most of the stores were now open and ready for the Saturday crowd. We watched the Wonder-bread truck unload its delivery to the grocery store across the avenue. The mailman passed, slipped some envelopes through the slot, waved, and moved on.

Finally I said, "Are you . . . sure Kendrick didn't do it?"

Bert's eyes narrowed and her lips grew thin and I knew if she could have tapped one of those hot straightening combs against my scalp she would have done so.

"I mean," I said quickly, "what are you going to do?"

She turned on the stool and seemed to fold into

herself as she spoke. "Girl, I don't even know where to start. What few coins I stashed, you know I'm willin' to spend . . ."

"But any attorney worth his fee is going to ask you the same thing: Did Kendrick shoot her? You were on the scene. You heard him say, 'I didn't mean it.' Why would he say that?"

"I don't know, but listen here: What I told you about Kendrick and Thea, I haven't mentioned to nobody else. As much as they questioned me, I didn't and wouldn't tell them cops shit. That's all them lazy, doughnut-eatin' sorry asses is lookin' for is an open-and-shut case. No offense 'cause you was once a cop yourself. But they ain't sendin' another black man upstate to be meat for them racist jail guards. It ain't gonna happen. He's my brother and I ain't gonna let it happen!"

"All right. All right. I was just asking. Just trying to . . ."

She turned away, and in the mirror I watched her raise the edge of the towel to her face and hold it there.

"Mali, what are they gonna do to him? Boy's twenty-six years old. I've looked after him since he was sixteen. After Mama died, between me and my daddy, he stayed straight. Daddy's gone so it's him and me. If he gets convicted, what's gonna happen? I can't even think . . ."

I left my chair to go stand at her side. I knew she had plenty to worry about. I could have told her that her brother didn't have to be sent upstate for bad things to happen. It could happen right here in my old precinct, or in the house of detention, or out at Rikers. No need to travel to be beaten or gang-raped or killed. And his damn good looks would only add to his problems. I didn't tell her that. Instead, I put my arm around her shoulder.

"Listen, Bertha: We're going to beat this . . . we're going to get Kendrick out." I realized I was making a promise I didn't know how to keep, but I had to find a way. And fast.

And Bertha was willing to put out every cent she had earned from her twelve-hour days. Sweating in the summer when the AC acted up and sometimes freezing in the winter until she managed to get the furnace working again. Days standing on her feet smiling while her favorite corn called her name out loud.

The shop had a steady stream of regulars, and she was familiar with the hurtful core of many lives: how a fancy hairdo might help to keep a man close; a different tint to attract a new one; a massage to the neck to deal with drunken blows to the head. Bert knew and kept her mouth shut and distracted them with the larger-than-life chaos of the TV soaps.

I watched her in the mirror as she wiped her eyes. They were red-rimmed and would probably get worse as more people dropped by to add their opinions to the news.

"I'll stay here, Bert. Run interference. Let everyone know that what happened last night is no one else's business. I could say it without you losing a customer."

She put the towel down and shook her head.

"No. It's probably all in the papers today. I have to handle this 'cause there's more to come. A lot more."

The warm water splashing against my scalp did not relax me. My eyes remained open and thoughts came fast and heavy. Last night Bert had heard footsteps. Then Thea's voice and the blast of the pistol. Where had Kendrick come from? What had he meant by his outburst? Who else could have been there? Who had made the call to get her out in the alley in the first place? Did Henderson Laws know that the light was out in the alley? Cheap as he was, he might've turned it off himself.

"Bert, why don't you close for the day?"

"I can't. Right now, I'm gonna need every dollar that come through that door."

And she was right. O.J.'s dream team was not available for what Bert was able to scrape together. I couldn't help her either because I was scheduled to start more graduate courses in September and I was working for my dad. He was doing well enough with his music to get himself incorporated. My salary would help pay my tuition.

The smell of coffee filled the shop and I sat under the dryer, gazing out the window onto Eighth Avenue.

Ex-cop. This street had once been my beat. It looked benign now as folks browsed and pushed shopping carts along the steaming sidewalk. Older folks tended to come out early to pick up groceries and gossip and get back home before the purse snatchers, the parasites who say they "gotta get paid," hit the streets.

This being the weekend, the later the hour, the younger the crowd. The club people were probably just turning over from last night's happenings at Mirage or the Tunnel and wouldn't be fully functional much before noon.

Still later, a different crew—the "pharmacists"—would take over with their bold pitches. "See me for Ecstasy. Black Tar? Yo. Stop the car! Step on over for Red Rover."

The labels changed every week, but the Black Tar Mexican heroin and the rock cocaine brought the same eager buyers cruising by in everything from Broncos to Benzes, and the crew stepped to the windows and filled orders more efficiently than at a fast-food takeout.

I thought of Kendrick and other young men like him who chose to look beyond the sucker dollars that the drug dealers worshipped, yet Kendrick was now in jail and the dealers were still outside, dealing, poisoning children as young as seven and eight years old. I thought of Alvin sailing aboard Captain Bo's schooner in St. Croix and was glad that we had someplace to send him for the summer. Though with him gone, the house at times seemed large and empty. Sometimes I even missed the window-rattling hip-hop sounds blasting from his room.

I studied the two business cards in my hand. Miss Ponytail's was elaborately designed with grand loops and curlicues around the raised lettering of "Gladys

Winston. Winston Associates Real Estate Sales and Management."

Her card and Blondie's had Manhattan phone numbers.

"I'll call both of them," I said, making up my mind to move fast. "But first, I need to speak to someone. Find out what's going on."

She looked at me and smiled for the first time. "You callin' Detective Honeywell, ain't you?"

"Maybe . . ."

"Damn. What a honey. I should be that lucky."

I did not answer. Maybe I wouldn't feel so lucky once he found out I was nosing in police business again. I reached for a notepad and jotted down a number.

"Here. Call my attorney. The thing is to move fast so Kendrick won't have to spend too much time in jail."

The word *jail* made her face crumple like old linen. I went to the door and flipped the CLOSED sign.

"Bertha, you're in no shape. Go upstairs. I'll call you as soon as I can."

I was surprised when she turned off the coffeemaker and picked up the keys without a word.

chapter three

Eighth Avenue seemed hard and bright after the dim coziness of the shop. The sun was directly overhead but most people didn't seem to notice. They moved quickly, ignoring the sonic waves from a boom box on a fire escape that sent ear-aching vibrations across the avenue.

I cut through 138th Street, where it was more quiet and less crowded, and strolled past number 257, where the office and factory of Black Swan Records once operated. Dad had pointed out the location, saying that Black Swan, in 1921, was the first record company in the United States owned by African-Americans. Ethel Waters had been their most important artist.

On Seventh Avenue, near the marquee of the old Renaissance Ballroom, a line of cars edged past the farm trucks, most of the cars slowing to discharge passengers who then made their way to the tables of produce set up under the marquee. Watermelons, collard greens, bas-

kets of peaches, yams, and string beans, and large
brown bags of paper-shell pecans brought brisk business. People also crowded around the tailgates of the
trucks for the smoked ham hocks, jars of honey, and
blackstrap molasses. The Renaissance Ballroom was
slated for renovation. When it reopened as a catering
hall, I wondered what would happen to these long haul-
ers and the folks who sometimes came all the way from
Brooklyn to buy the Southern yams and smoked pig-
tails.

On the next few blocks, despite the heat, double-
Dutch teams of young girls were in business with ropes
slapping fast and serious against the pavement. Hoop
players had staked out several squares of concrete from
stoop to curb and aimed high for the cut-out milk crate
tied to the tree.

The stoop watchers were out also, lounging on
whatever was at hand—mostly the abundant milk
crates amid a scattering of unsteady plastic chairs. The
super of one building, Old Man Johnson, who was per-
fectly able to walk, lounged with legs crossed in a dis-
carded wheelchair, biting on a dead cigar. They sat in
front of houses splintering from decay, busily watching
the rhythm and action curling past them, calling loudly
to passersby and to one another and waving and laughing and oblivious to last night's happening.

On the lot where Better Crust Pie Shop and the
Dawn Casino and Stone's Tire Repair Shop had once
stood, a line of cars inched forward at Mickey Dee's
takeout. Among them was a battered red van with a
large FOR SALE sign taped to its fender. On its dust-

coated windows, someone had finger-inscribed in much larger print: FIRST PLEASE WASH MY ASS.

Diagonally across from Mickey Dee's, at 140th Street, the door of the Half-Moon was in motion. I glanced at my watch. It was noon, less than twelve hours after the murder of one of his employees, and it seemed that Henderson Laws had nothing better to do than to reopen for business.

On the side street, someone had placed a bunch of roses and a candle near the police tape that was blocking the alley. People walking by paused. Some went inside the bar, others moved on.

I went inside. The place was long and narrow with an oak bar and a mirrored wall behind it. The booths near the brick wall opposite the counter were filled with nearly everyone from the neighborhood.

The lights had been turned off and I had to pause to get my bearings. Only the small neon crescent over the register was lit, and flickering in the dark were more candles than I'd seen at a High Mass. Votives placed among the tiers of liquor refracted the red, brown, and amber casts of the bottles.

At the counter, the crowd leaned elbow to elbow, dipping into platters of chicken, ribs, greens, salad, and rolls.

I moved farther in and saw that the solid stuff was gratis but the liquid was not, and the ring of the cash register cut through the noise like an Atlantic City slot machine.

. . . A paying wake. That crafty 'bajan was holding a paying wake for one of his own employees. I knew he had a knack for a nickel, but damn . . .

Henderson Laws was short and slim and still spoke with the faint trace of an island accent, although he had been in Harlem nearly thirty years. At fifty-something, his dark skin was still unlined and he sported a silver goatee shaved to an arrow below his lower lip, which reminded me of spittle he had somehow neglected to wipe away. Despite this, he might have been called handsome except for the tendency of his left eye to cross every now and then. Anyone else might have felt handicapped but Laws used it like he used everything else in his life: With his "floating eye," as he called it, he'd stand at one end of the bar, gaze at the other end, and nobody would really know which way he was looking. That kept the bartender's fingers straight and also kept folks from staring too closely at his toupee, which always seemed a little lopsided to me.

He was leaning now in his favorite spot near the end of the bar, watching the platters move through the swinging door. He nodded and sighed heavily when someone approached to shake his hand or touch his shoulder in sympathy, but the good eye remained trained on the register.

The counter had twelve stools, and the two new barkeeps, pressed into sudden service, struggled to keep up with the orders.

TooHot, the numbers runner, sat on a stool nearest the window, watching a small mountain of slips expanding before him. Everyone, it seemed, was "combinating" 967—the number for the dead—though

I heard a few other digits floating in the air, probably Thea's address or variations on her phone number.

"Gimme another Walker Black," TooHot yelled, rapping his finely manicured fingers on the counter. He pushed his panama away from his brown face, bit into a chicken wing, and allowed the slips to pile up, knowing that the cops would think twice before busting a wake. He was dressed appropriately for the occasion in a dark gray silk suit and black shirt.

More people pushed in and I wondered if it was the food, the numbers, or the sympathy that brought them. Familiar faces called to me from the booths, but there was no one I wanted to slide into conversation with except TooHot, and he was too busy.

I scanned the bar trying to figure who might have been on the scene last night. I spotted Jesse Long still sporting his gray Elvis sideburns and denim bell-bottoms that were so old they were new again. He had angled a strategic spot next to Big-Time Colloway, who was busy setting up the bar. Big-Time was a Rikers guard who bragged about his "heavy dime from over-time," yet rumor had it that he'd cussed his own mama when she demanded he pay room and board. He and Jesse now wiped out a platter between them and reached for a new one. I guessed that Jesse was filling up on enough greens and potato salad to last until the food stamps rolled in, but Big-Time—who had a job— was putting away enough for three starving people.

It was likely that both had been here last night, but I didn't approach them because Jesse would proba-bly want a drink and Big Time, an NYPD wanna-be, would want to flash his latest pay stub and crack on the fact that I was no longer on the force, a big thing in his world.

Someone turned on the jukebox and the uproar retreated somewhere behind the cry of Whitney Houston.

The heat from the open candles and press of the crowd was beginning to get to me. I would have to catch TooHot another time, perhaps when he passed by Bertha's place. I turned to leave but I felt a light touch on my arm.

"Good morning. Care for a drink?"

Detective Lieutenant Tad Honeywell pressed against me, using the crowd as an excuse. I glanced up into eyes that even in this darkness resembled heavy smoke. He was casually dressed in a beige silk shirt and dark brown herringbone linen slacks. I took in his soft deliberate expression, which reminded me of the midnights on his terrace.

"Absolut and orange?" he whispered.

"No thanks. I—it's too early."

Not only was it too early for a drink but it was too early to be feeling this unsteady on my feet. Which happened every time I saw him.

"It's twelve noon."

"I know, but I had a hard night."

"That," he whispered, "is because you didn't spend it with me."

I gazed at him, beginning to really feel the heat. I was having a hard time breathing, concentrating. I got like that sometimes. At other times, when he touched me, I had to sit or lie down.

"It—it's warm in here," I whispered. "Let's step outside."

He nodded and I followed him through the crowd. As we passed TooHot he held out his hand and whispered.

"Say, Lieutenant. Great job y'all did on that crew uptown. Cleaned up things pretty good 'round here."

"We try. We try . . . ," Tad said, staring pointedly at the pile of slips on the counter.

TooHot ignored the look and tipped his five-hundred-dollar panama to me. "And how you doin', Miss Mali? How's your dad? Saw him at the club the other night. Still kickin' it."

"Yes, he is." I smiled.

"Great job, Lieutenant," he said again, tipping his hat higher. I smiled because I knew what he really meant: Since that notorious drug enterprise had been busted and several cops had gone down with the gang, the spotlight was hot on the precinct now, so strong in fact that every cop in Harlem was walking with his shield pinned on straight—and TooHot wasn't under pressure to pay his weekly "social security" ("secure us and we'll be social" was the way some poet at the precinct had put it to him).

Lately, TooHot had been able to keep that extra thousand dollars a week in his pocket, and he was making the most of the temporary lull. And Thea's passing, unfortunate as it was, created another spike in earnings.

So here he was, taking advantage of what circumstances had thrown his way.

Outside in the street, I shook my head. "No respect. That man has no respect."

Tad shrugged. "Well, he's how old—seventy, seventy-one? What else is he going to do?"

"He could retire. He certainly has enough money. A duplex condo in St. Thomas ain't cheap."

The tape stretched like a plastic snake across the alley, and the single offering of roses had grown to include carnations, a pot of never-dies, and a fragile wisp of baby's breath enclosed in an irregular semicircle of candles. The roses had already begun to wilt from the heat jetting like ribbons from the stained pavement.

"How come you're in the Half-Moon? And so early?"

I shrugged at the question. It was just like Tad to veer from one topic to another. It worked with the suspects, but it always caught me off guard and I found it annoying.

"You know Bert's my friend," I reminded him. "And Kendrick's her brother. She's trying to figure out what happened."

"But she was here last night," he answered, holding his gaze steady. "You weren't."

I shaded my eyes and leaned against the car, debating whether I should remind Tad how Kendrick had stepped in and helped Alvin—and me—after my sister had died. And he'd had a hundred other things to do—he didn't have to help me, but he did . . .

"Damned good-lookin' brother," Tad went on.

Lord, so are you, I wanted to say. I glanced up, smiling, ready to tell him so, but the look in his eyes stopped me cold. I was amazed. We stood there in the July heat, looking everywhere now but at each other. It was one of those silences that should have remained unbroken but I had to say what was on my mind.

"Tad! For heaven's sake, I'm not interested. Kendrick's like a brother to me. A kid brother. He's a child, a boy!" I emphasized *child* and *boy* and didn't mention *man,* but that didn't cool the temperature rising behind Tad's eyes.

"Kendrick's not a boy. He's not a child. He's a good-looking twenty-six-year-old man."

"He's six years younger than me, for God's sake!"

"And I'm eight years older than you, Mali. Age is just a number, up or down."

I closed my eyes and said no more, hoping this stupid conversation would blow away on the wind. Last year, he'd been jealous of a dead man. Now here he was acting crazy because of a . . . boy. Well, let him think what he wanted to. I owed Kendrick something.

Finally he sighed and I knew word-for-word what was coming.

"Mali, remember the last time you stuck your neck out, you nearly lost it."

I did not answer, remembering everything from last summer: the odor of that crackhouse; the handcuffs biting into my skin; a .38 fired so near my ear I was dizzy for days after. And the body count. I would have been one of those bodies if it hadn't been for Tad. If he had stepped out on that roof a second later, I'd have gone down with a bullet in my face.

"Listen, Mali: Bert is your friend, but let the department handle this, okay?"

I concentrated on the police tape and did not answer. Seventh Avenue was busy and more passersby paused to look. An old woman made the sign of the cross and murmured something too soft for me to hear.

Tad cleared his throat and veered again.

"So, how often did Kendrick stop by the shop?"

"Often enough," I said, trying to keep my tone neutral.

"I understand he's a model . . ."

"Yes."

"And an actor."

"Yes."

"Is he planning to have his ear pierced?"

"Who knows?" I said, beginning to feel really annoyed. "So what if he is? Every other brother and his father these days has his ear, nose, or navel ringed. What are you saying . . . ?"

"Nothing. Just trying to figure his taste in jewelry."

"You planning to give him a present?"

"Maybe. Maybe not. We found a small stud earring near the body. Square-cut diamond. Very high-quality stone. That one earring is probably worth nearly two thousand dollars."

I whistled. Two thousand dollars was a lot of earring for a struggling actor, but it probably wasn't his.

Bert said the alley had been so jammed she couldn't move, so the earring could have belonged to anyone.

"I don't know what his plans were and I'm not familiar with his taste in jewelry," I said. "All I know is he dressed well, looked good"—and added for good measure—"and he was very much in love with Thea."

He looked at me and there was a pause before he spoke. "Love. Mm-hmm. Love. It'll undo you every time."

He said it with a soft singsong rhythm but I heard the bitter undercurrent, and it was like glimpsing a sudden flare on a dark horizon. Brief, natural, and dangerous. I quickly changed the subject.

"What else did you find?"

"She had her own earrings on. A .45 slug shattered her nose and right cheekbone and exited the back of her skull."

"A .45. I didn't think anyone bothered with those anymore. Must be a museum piece."

"May be old but it did the job. Took most of her face and all of the back of her skull completely away."

"Was the weapon recovered?"

"Not yet. There were a lot of people in the alley before we got there. Bert was battling Laws. People were trying to break that up. Some were trying to help Thea. There was so much confusion anyone could've scooped it and walked. Piece like that'll still get a good price on the market."

I frowned. Then I watched as Tad's fingers slid over the door handle of his car, but I made no move to get in. As much as I wanted—needed—to be with him, I also needed to see how Bert was holding up.

Tad's voice, much softer now, interrupted my thoughts: "You know, I haven't seen you in a while."

"Last Friday night," I murmured, gazing up at him. He was six foot three and his brown skin seemed to glow in the noon heat.

"Last Friday," he repeated. "Baby, that's seven days. Seven days too long."

He stepped closer and I looked up, catching the wisp of mint as he whispered, "How about tonight?"

"What time?" I whispered, hoping he'd say, What about right now?

"Nine?"

The slight smile deepened and I felt the sweat gather in the small of my back. I reached for his hand, which was hot against the metal of the car. I wanted to touch his mouth but he was gazing beyond me at the flowers on the pavement.

His fingers brushed somewhere near my ear and he spoke again, voice still low. "You know how I feel about you, girl. See you tonight. Remember what I said. Let the department handle this."

Then he was in the car and pulling away from the curb. Fast. Before I could consider what was really the issue. "Let the department handle it."

By that he meant "stay away from the brother."

chapter four

I went home instead of returning to the shop. Dad was in the living room, his six-foot frame stretched the length of the sofa and pages of the *Daily Challenge* spread on the floor beside him. Ruffin was stretched out on the cool tiles in front of the fireplace.

Both of them sat up when I walked in. "Bertha called three times. She's upset. Got every right to be. This thing's in all the papers. Even on WINS. I can't believe this. Thea. Gone just like that, and they blamin' it on Kendrick, of all people."

He laid the page flat on his lap and folded his arms across it, as if to close out the news it contained.

"I know, Dad. I know. And please, when Alvin calls tonight, don't mention anything about this."

He was upset and didn't answer. I thought of fixing him a gin and tonic but today was Saturday: He had a full schedule of students coming and never took a drink or allowed anything else to interfere with his music or his music lessons.

I moved over and disengaged the paper.

FORMER NEW YORK STATE BEAUTY CONTESTANT SLAIN.

"Thea Morris, 33-year-old singer and former beauty-pageant finalist, was shot to death early this morning in an alley adjoining the Half-Moon Bar on West 140th Street in Harlem. The lounge crowd had gathered to celebrate her birthday, and police sources believe she may have been killed over a love affair gone wrong. An aspiring actor, 26-year-old Kendrick Owen, was arrested at the scene. Bertha Owen, the suspect's sister and proprietor of a local beauty shop, was also questioned at the scene. 'My brother wouldn't do this,' she said. 'He's not the type.' "

I put the paper down. "A love affair gone wrong. The end."

Dad took the page and tore out the article, intending to save it. "I don't know about that. Seems like the cops movin' too fast on this one. They oughtta go talk to that Michaels guy before they wrap it up."

"Edwin Michaels? Why?"

" 'Cause one of my buddies was just here—you remember Jackson, killer on the sax. Left just before you came in. Anyway, he was in the Half-Moon last night. Dropped by to see what was happenin'. Said Michaels was there and when he wasn't pressin' a palm he was pressin' as close behind Thea as he could get. Had that hangdog look on his face—like he was glad for any bone she threw his way."

"What? Irresistible, ultraconservative, family-values—Edwin Michaels?" I laughed at the idea. "What else did Jackson see?"

"Nuthin'. He had a gig and left before the bullets started flyin', but I'll tell you somethin' else."

He moved to clear the rest of the papers off the floor. His first lesson was due in five minutes.

"Thea had a lotta gigs at the club and Michaels was front-row every night, all night. He would chill at first, but after a couple a rounds, he would be hawkin' worse than one a them starvin' street dudes you see with their faces pressed to restaurant windows. Never seen nuthin' like it. Big-time politician. Nice wife. Kid in college. And he let that girl open his nose wide enough to roll his Benz through."

"Well," I said, "she *was* pretty."

"Yes she was." He checked his watch and picked up a stack of sheet music from the coffee table. "She was pretty. But whatever a person has, don't mean diddly if she doesn't do something with it. She coulda been a great singer. Everybody in the band saw that, but she could never get beyond that certain level, push herself across that threshold. Something—I don't know what, it was like somebody's hand was holdin' her shoulder and she couldn't shake it off. She was pretty, but so what . . ."

He headed downstairs to his study and Ruffin followed, leaving me alone in the living room.

. . . So what indeed. And voice or no voice, if Thea had Kendrick, seven years younger than she, and Michaels, the original satisfier of desire—if she had

them turned on like that, she probably had a few more
licking in her pot. Whatever turned on those men, caus-
ing them to act like fools, that talent didn't limit itself to
just two men. That thing, whatever it was, had a tendency to spread itself out.

I wondered about my own feelings, about this current of envy simmering inside me. Why was I jealous of
a dead woman? Especially considering the way she had
died. And it was hard not to admit that when I'd heard
the news, I'd felt sorrier for Kendrick than I had for
her.

I curled up on the sofa, trying to understand what
I was feeling and remembering a long time ago, when
Dad had spoken of another woman like Thea.

*"Because of Lettie," he said to us one morning, my mother,
sister, and I listening as we ate breakfast and asked why the
famous band he had traveled with had suddenly broken up.*

*"Now Lettie," he said, "was short and shapely and
had a mean set a pipes but she was no knockout—at least
not when it came to her looks. But every town and city we
hit—large, small, and in between—that woman had the
men coming out from everywhere except the cemetery. They
came in overalls, business suits, and preacher's collars. I
mean wallets and pants snapped open. House deeds and car
keys fell on her like rain. This is a time when blacks folks is
struggling . . .*

*"And she wasn't a whore or prostitute. She never
made a move or held out her hand, yet that thing, whatever
it was, seemed to float out of her. Like sweet sweat. Earned*

the woman more money than the whole damn band was pullin' down."

"When did she find time to sing?" my mother asked, looking at him levelly over the slice of toast she had raised to her small mouth. "Wasn't she . . . a bit tired?"

Dad lifted his shoulders and I half-expected—hoped—he would wink at Mom, so she would widen her mouth into a smile once again, but he didn't seem to notice and went on matter-of-factly. Like he was a reporter or something.

"Most of the time, she sorta leaned against the piano. And those satin gowns, when the light hit the right way, seemed to move even when she didn't. She just rested and riffed. Of course, when she did that more than a couple a times, the piano player got to thinkin' maybe he could play her as well as the piano. Causin' the horn man to cop an unnecessary attitude. In the end, she broke up the whole damn band. Nice bunch a guys, but she busted it . . .

"Heard she went to Frisco. Doin' a solo thing in her own club. And livin' in a big mansion."

He'd told that story a long time ago, when I was just old enough to listen to such stories but too young to ask if he himself had been pulled into Lettie's "thing." I never found out, but I never forgot, and I had harbored a deep and secret admiration for Lettie ever since.

Thea seemed to have what Lettie had, but I did not admire her. I did not like her.

At the Club Harlem last summer, Dad had brought her to the table after a set and introduced me.

Thea was then in the end stage of her Diana Ross incarnation, and since there had been no wind machine to do the job, she was occupied with brushing at least a pound of weave from over her left eye alone. When she'd finally extended her hand, it was as thin and brittle as her smile.

"So you're Jeffrey's daughter. I've seen you at Bertha's shop." The word *Jeffrey* held a proprietary ring, as if Jeffrey was her man and she'd just discovered he had relatives. Shit, the man was my father.

She had also stared at my two-inch afro as if it was the first one she'd ever seen. I didn't try to figure out her bad attitude. Instead, I flashed her my happy-I'm-nappy smile, kissed my father on the cheek, and made up my mind to say no more than hello when she popped in to Bert's to get her bird's nest tightened up.

The bell rang now and I moved from the sofa to open the door. Morris, my nephew's friend, had arrived on schedule.

"How's Alvin?" he asked as he and his mother stepped in.

"Wait a minute," Mrs. Johnson said. "Don't you know how to say hello first?"

"I'm sorry. How are you, Miss Mali? When is Alvin coming home? He still in St. Croix sailin' on that boat?"

"He'll be back in a few weeks," I said, touching his shoulder and pointing downstairs. His mother handed him his trumpet case. "See you in an hour, Morris, and you mind your manners."

The boy headed downstairs, grumbling, "Sure be glad when Alvin get back. Nobody to play ball with."

When he was out of sight, Mrs. Johnson whispered, "Ain't it somethin' about that girl at the Half-Moon? I heard her sing a couple a times. She was damn good. Too bad she had to go that way."

When the door closed, I did not return to the sofa. Dredging up old memories wasn't helping. Thea was dead, Kendrick was in jail, and somebody needed to find out who'd killed her.

chapter five

either Teddi Lovette nor Gladys Winston answered when I called. I left messages and then phoned Bertha. She came on sounding as if all the breath had been blown out of her.

"Bert, what happened?"

"I tried callin' down to Centre Street, but they couldn't or wouldn't tell me anything. Then when I hung up, the phone rang and Elizabeth Jackson, the lawyer you recommended? She was down there, said Kendrick was in a fight. Somebody tried to . . . bother with him, she said. So he had to defend himself."

I couldn't believe it. Kendrick was still in the holding cell. He hadn't even been arraigned yet and someone was eyeing him already.

"Was he hurt?"

"Oh no. Lotta people don't know he's a black belt. They find out when it's too late."

"Did she say when he'd be arraigned?"

"Monday."

"Don't worry about Kendrick too much. He knows how to take care of himself."

I hung up, thankful that Bert had no idea what the holding pen looked like: a huge, barred cage crammed with hardballs; one bench to sit on; one toilet not to sit on. Men throwing up. Cursing. Threatening to cut your throat if you blinked the wrong way. People sometimes had to wait as long as seventy-two hours before they were arraigned. And of course Kendrick was not going to cop a plea, so no bail and a trip to Rikers was coming up. His black belt would come in handy.

Kendrick was tall, about six foot one, with skin like melted chocolate, and his deep-set eyes and even teeth were enough to make a nun give up her vows. I hadn't realized the impact he had on women until the day Bertha remarked, "Seems like my business tripled since Kendrick started givin' out my cards. He's some salesman."

Indeed he is, I'd thought. And Alvin had mentioned instances of young women walking up to Kendrick in the street and introducing themselves, or simply falling in front of him while in-line skating.

I thought about what he had said in the alley: "*I didn't mean it . . .*"

I closed my eyes, trying to imagine the sound of his voice.

Mean what? Had somebody scooped the weapon or had Kendrick set her up and the killer walked off with the gun?

I was getting dressed, intending to drop by Bertha's place, when the phone rang.

"Mali Anderson? This is Gladys Winston."

Her voice was strong and confident, as if she'd called to interest me in a choice parcel of real estate. "How are you?"

"I'm fine. I want to apologize again for Kendrick's sister. She's extremely upset by Thea's death—as we all are."

"I know. I still can't understand how something like this could've—I just don't understand . . ."

I paused for a respectful second of silence, then said, "I'd like to meet with you, to talk about this. It's no good asking questions over the phone."

It was her turn to pause, and when she spoke some of the confidence had slipped away. "What sort of questions?"

"Well, Bertha doesn't believe Kendrick did it . . ."

"Quite naturally. She's his sister."

"No. I mean she was there and—"

"Well, okay. We may as well get this over with. When are you available?"

"Well—right now, if it's okay with you."

"Fine. Come to my office. You have my card."

She hung up before I could say good-bye.

It was 6 P.M., plenty of time to see Gladys and still get to Tad's place by 9. That was one date I meant to keep. This no-cal, no-fat love life had me talking in my sleep.

• • •

Gladys Winston worked in a large three-desk office on Fifth Avenue near 125th Street one floor above a fabric store run by a Senegalese couple. The voices of the customers, in English and Wolof, followed me into the adjoining entrance hall and up the stairs to the second floor. Before I touched the bell, Gladys Winston opened the door.

"Saw you from the window," she said, motioning me to a large desk in the corner. The office was well furnished with two smaller desks facing each other in the center of the carpeted room and low mahogany file cabinets lining one wall. The beginnings of a western sunset cast a strong orange tint on the plants in the wide window and a vertical fish tank that stood in the corner. Large framed pictures of Harlem brownstones on tree-lined blocks—some of which I recognized were on Convent Avenue—lined the beige walls.

Gladys's desk was separated by a waist-high Plexiglas partition. She sat down opposite me and eased her feet out of her shoes. The red Chanel suit jacket that was draped over the chair told me everything I needed to know about her sales commissions. Her ponytail was now twisted into a French knot, and her face, when she wasn't frowning, was actually pretty. She was probably in her mid-thirties, but right now her drawn face made her appear older.

"It's been tough." She sighed. "I couldn't work, couldn't concentrate. Susan and Margie, my two brokers, are out, showing houses, and I've turned the machine on because I need this quiet time. Perhaps by Monday I'll feel like my old self again."

She waved her hand toward the computers on the desk. "Right now, I'm completely out of it."

She walked over to one of the cabinets, her bare feet soundless on the thick carpet, and returned with a quart of Absolut and a bottle of ginger ale.

"Sorry. Our ice maker's acting up. Haven't seen a cube in a week now. Hope you don't mind." She placed two glasses on the desk and poured. "We pull this out on celebratory occasions—a half-million contract, a multiple closing, whatever. We offer a toast."

She raised her glass and suddenly put it down. Then picked it up again and closed her eyes. "Well, Thea. We had fun . . ."

Feeling like a hypocrite, I sighed and lifted my own glass. But the toast was a good opening.

"How long had you known Thea?"

"Let's see . . ." Gladys had gone light on the ginger ale and the drink made her cough. She held her breath until the initial burning subsided. "Let's see. We met at the pageant in 1985. In Albany. She was first runner-up and I was second. She should've won, but . . ."

"But what?"

Gladys shrugged, changing the subject as if she had not heard me. "We shared a suite. There were so many chaperones, you wouldn't believe. We couldn't smoke, drink, chew gum. Not that we wanted to, you understand, and I think Thea was a little more

driven—motivated—than I was, at least in the beginning."

I nodded, not certain if it was the Absolut or the
well of memory, but she seemed suddenly animated.
Her mouth curved into a small smile and she seemed
even younger.

"Thea was twenty-one and I was twenty-three,"
she said, "and we wanted everything to be picture perfect, so chewing and drinking were the least of our
problems. I mean we went through all the phases of the
competition—talent, swimsuit, evening wear. Every
curl in place and the smiles pasted on. We were gorgeous. Here, look."

She reached into the bottom drawer and pulled
out a thick album held together with a swath of black-
and-white kente cloth. The pictures were not fastened
in place and spilled out when she opened the cover.

I studied them, mostly eight-by-tens. The 1985
Thea had paler skin; the smile was softer, more expec-
tant; but there was something around the eyes that the
smile couldn't hide.

"Were these taken before or after the winners
were announced?"

Gladys put on her glasses and leaned over. "These
were taken before." She paused and sighed. "They
hadn't yet decided that we weren't quite good enough."

I looked at her quickly. She was pouring a second
drink and I wondered if she'd had any before I'd shown
up.

"The gowns must've cost a fortune," I said.

"Not only the gowns," Gladys said, gathering the

pictures and putting them back in the album. "That doesn't begin to explain the price we paid. You see, every contestant had to have a sponsor, someone to underwrite expenses. My church and my family had sponsored me, and Thea's voice coach had sponsored her . . ."

"Her voice coach? Where was her family?"

Gladys lifted her shoulders again. "In all the years I've known her, that's one area I could never get into. She always seemed angry whenever I mentioned my mother, or my aunt, or cousins.

"My family had been in real estate for years, and I was already planning to enter the business. I didn't need a beauty title as a stepping-stone. My future was mapped. Five years ago, when my dad retired, I took over. Thea didn't have that kind of backup. If you ask me, she seemed to not have any security at all, except her grandmother, who'd taken ill, and Thea flew home for a day to see her. The only calls she received were from her voice coach.

"The day before we returned to the city, the grandmother died. I dropped by Thea's place from time to time, but there were no pictures of family. No albums. It was as if she'd been dropped from another planet to make out here as best she could. One thing I must say: She was gorgeous, but even with that I didn't envy her. Most of the time she was angry, and I never understood that."

She returned the album to the bottom drawer. "And that's the personal side. At that pageant, there was a lot of pressure. Publicly, we had to keep our cool when some redneck cow from one of those one-light towns tried to flaunt her whiteness in our faces, tried in so many words to call us out of our names, smiling as she did it. We had to smile back, grit our teeth, and work hard to keep from acting colored, so to speak."

"How did Thea take it?"

"Early on, she was determined to grit and grin. But then the cows turned up the heat. I'm telling you, there were some slick heifers behind all that lipstick. They tried things like hiding or destroying parts of our wardrobe, shoes, music, makeup, anything to make us misstep, miss a note, sweat, frown at the wrong time . . ."

"Losing must have been hard for Thea."

"Yes, toward the end she was crying every night, all night, and in the morning I would put ice packs on her eyes to reduce the swelling and redness. I kept telling her not to let those fat cows get to her. After a while, though, I wondered if it was the cows or the fact that no one was there to support her, no family to back her up . . ."

"Who's her voice coach?"

"Miss Adele. You know her. Everyone in Harlem knows her. Retired from the Met and pulled a lot of weight downtown. Lived in the Dunbar Apartments years ago but she's across Seventh Avenue in Esplanade Gardens now. She's in her seventies and still going strong, still coaching. A remarkable woman."

I nodded. Her name sounded vaguely familiar. I'd have to ask Dad more about her. Anyone having the slightest connection to the music scene—even if they only whistled their way through the *Apollo Amateur Hour* without being booed off the stage—Dad either knew or had heard of.

"How often did you see Thea?"

"About every month or so. She was modeling, singing. We called each other quite a lot, probably because she had no one else to confide in."

"Who's handling the funeral arrangements?"

"I suppose I'll do it. Her husband—"

"Husband? Thea was married?"

"Yes, in 1991, but Roger had left her. Wanted a divorce, but she refused for some reason. I couldn't understand that."

"Did she love him?"

She picked up her glass again, twirled it from habit, then put it down. "I don't know. They met when she was modeling. Married quickly and broke up just as fast. I mean before the wedding pictures came from the photographer she was back in her apartment on 116th Street and Seventh Avenue."

"Graham Court?"

"Yes. I was glad she hadn't given that up. In some ways, the girl was smart. Place has seven large rooms, beautiful fireplaces, fabulous floors."

Gladys looked at me, aware that she had slipped momentarily into her broker's role.

"Then she demanded a settlement. A very expensive one. Roger's a successful architect and I suppose Thea thought he should meet her price. Personally, I was disappointed. Roger could have given her the love and security she seemed to need so badly."

The smile had vanished and Gladys seemed ready to cry, so I remained quiet as she refilled the glasses. Alcohol usually loosens the tongue, but if tears came there might be no more conversation. She had turned the answering machine down but not entirely off and several messages—more like murmurs—filtered into the silence. Gladys ignored them and I remained silent, thinking about Thea.

Damn. The girl had been married. Not even the papers mentioned that. Dad, who knew all about everyone in the business, didn't mention that. It must have truly been one of those blink-and-you-miss-it moments.

"If I'm not being too inquisitive, how much was Thea asking to cut this guy loose?"

Gladys looked at her watch, a paper-thin gold Piaget, and rose to get another bottle of ginger ale. She moved toward the small refrigerator and her voice when she answered trailed after her. "The last figure I heard was around fifty thousand. That was three years ago. She suggested he could pay it in installments."

Installments. How thoughtful. And not a bad pay-off for a few months' inconvenience. Whatever the hell was wrong with her, the girl was definitely a high-maintenance sister.

Gladys must have anticipated my next question.

"I called his office as soon as I heard about Thea," she said. "Roger is in Puerto Rico at a conference."

"A conference. Out of town."

"Out of the country, actually."

"I see . . ."

I also saw that it was one thing to pay fifty thousand for your freedom. And quite a bargain to perhaps pay someone—when you were off the scene—five thousand to do a job for you. Maybe get it done for as little as five hundred if your connections were good. A crackhead might do it for fifty. Except they couldn't be trusted. If Roger had hired someone, it would've been a professional. But why wait so many years to do it? And why kill her on her birthday?

"When did you last speak to her?" I asked.

I watched her carefully as her eyes filled again, but the tears did not spill over. It was a few seconds before she said, "I talked to her shortly before she died. Called the bar to tell her I was on my way. I had been working on a closing late into the evening. When I got there, the place was in chaos. The police hadn't even roped it off yet. There were people, two women I think, still in the place . . ."

"Drinking?" I asked.

Gladys shook her head. "I don't know. I don't remember. I only remember hearing Kendrick's name. And I saw his sister, Bertha, screaming at the police, at Laws, at anybody who'd listen."

"Speaking of Bertha: Do you know the two women who came into her shop when you were there?"

She looked at me and shrugged. "I have no idea who they were. I was so upset I barely noticed them." She touched her forehead and closed her eyes. "Wait. Wait a minute. Yes. One of the women, the dark pretty one, had been in the bar when I walked in. There was another woman with her at the counter who was short, a bit on the heavy side, light brown complexion with a head full of thick hair that didn't seem to do much for her face. I remember the hair falling over her face and practically covering her eyeglasses. Strange, the things you remember . . .

"The glasses had rhinestone frames, and I remember thinking how tacky they looked. Can you imagine thinking about something so insignificant at a time like that?"

"I can imagine," I said. "Rhinestones can make a statement. Did you notice anything else?"

"No."

"What about the other woman? The white one?"

"I have no idea who she is."

Gladys rose to clear away the glasses and I looked toward the window. The sun had moved beyond the ridge of buildings across the avenue, and purplish shadows were easing into the room. Gladys pressed a button and plant lights flickered on in the window, bathing the front of the office in a surreal chalky white glow. In the artificial light, the fish in the narrow tank seemed to trail a bubbling phosphorescence as they moved through the water. The rest of the room remained in semidarkness. I checked my watch, a modest Timex, which read nearly 7:30.

"I suppose I'll see you at the service," she said.

Her voice had changed again, gotten softer, and I glanced at her and wondered how long she'd sit here after I left. Her eyes were still watery, but at least she had put the bottle back.

"Of course," I said. "She sang with my father's band."

chapter six

Outside, the shadows gave way to vivid strands of pink and yellow and glimmered in an uneven wedge above the buildings' silhouettes.

Ben and Jerry's Ice Cream Parlor on the corner of Fifth Avenue and 125th Street was crowded. Across the street, the National Black Theater was open, and a few doors away on Fifth, people strolled in and out of the Africarts Gallery.

I turned at 126th Street and headed west toward Lenox Avenue. This block, like many others in Harlem, was a study in contrasts where magnificent four-story brownstones stood side by side with structures long vacant. On the top floors of the vacant buildings, ubiquitous "city palms" had somehow taken root and their thin trunks spiraled toward the twilit sky. The broad-leaved branches jutted out of the yawning windows, waving like tenants in the yellow flare of the streetlight. I wondered who owned these buildings and how much longer they would be held off the market. Trees took years to grow.

At Lenox Avenue I walked uptown, thinking of the view from Tad's balcony in the Riverbend Apartments complex, seeing in my mind's eye early-morning sunlight on the Harlem River and feeling the wind damp against my skin. I imagined the small whoosh of water rushing to close in on itself in the wake of a passing barge and the dark current settling into a pattern again, easing and ebbing and waiting for the next boat to disturb it. I needed to speak to him.

I paused at a bodega and waited under its Christmas-lit canopy for a young girl to run out of quarters and free up the phone. Her conversation must have taken a turn because her free hand flipped to her hip and her neck went into the classic swan boogie. "Listen, you think I'm sweatin' you? Negro, lemme put this to you: By the time I get there you better have that bitch's ass in the wind, you hear? Yeah. Tell me somethin' new. She'd fuck a lamppost if it had a dick. Yeah . . . same to you and your mama too!"

With that she slammed down the phone and turned to me with a stare that could have cut stone. "Got that low-budget ho' in his crib. Ain't good for nuthin' but chokin'. Lucky I got my fuckin' other man."

I shrugged in sympathy, remembering when my younger hair-trigger temper had caused me to act just as foolishly. I remembered that when I wasn't screaming, I was crying, wearing out the grooves on "Love Don't Love Nobody" by the Spinners and "Kiss and Say

Goodbye" by the Manhattans, two anthems for every love that had ever gone wrong.

I wanted to tell this girl that nothing has changed but that she will change, cool out in six months, and laugh at this. But right now she was moving down the street, cloaked in righteous anger. I waited another minute for the mouthpiece to cool off before I lifted it and dialed.

Tad came on before the ring was completed.

"Mali, where are you?"

"128th and Lenox."

"Want me to pick you up?"

His apartment was at 140th Street and Fifth Avenue, really not that far away. I could get there blindfolded.

"No," I said. "I need to walk. I can think better when I'm walking."

"What's on your mind?"

"Nothing much. I love you, Baby. See you in a few minutes."

I hung up, slightly unnerved by the nagging feeling that he still had not gotten over his experience with Ellen, his ex-wife. Finding her in a compromising circumstance with another woman was bad enough, but when the shock had worn off, a wariness had set in that had remained to cast a shadow over our own relationship. In addition, his partner on the job, in whom he'd entrusted his life, had fallen for the big coke buck last summer and had betrayed Tad and the job.

The thing with Ellen had happened over two years earlier, yet when I was with Tad I trod softly, gauging his moods, listening to my words and his responses, and thankful for the moments of free-flowing feeling. Not only when we loved, but after, like when he would bury his head in the curve of my neck, and I would hear the slow, satisfied rhythm of his breathing.

I also tried not to mention Erskin Harding, the director of the Uptown Children's Chorus, who was murdered last summer. Tad thought I'd been involved with Erskin. Now if he knew I was still nosing around trying to find out about Thea, still trying to help Kendrick . . .

I continued to walk, wondering how to handle this. I'd have to tell him eventually, but right now all I wanted to do was stretch out on his terrace and feel his hands smoothing away all the little aches and pains.

At the next corner I dialed Bertha, and on the fourth ring I heard her voice thick with sleep.

"Mali? Girl, I was tired. So much stuff runnin' 'round in my brain, feel like it's herbed out. I can hardly think straight. I had to lay down . . . get myself together."

"How do you feel now?"

"A little better."

I was not convinced. "Listen, Bert: Monday, I'm coming with you. Bring a change of clothing for Kendrick. Elizabeth'll probably want to take the shirt and vest that he's wearing . . ."

"Now they strippin' 'im? What for?"

"To have the clothing tested, analyzed for traces of powder."

"They can do that?" Her voice lifted hopefully.

"They can do a lot of things, Bert."

She said nothing more but I heard the sigh of relief and decided to end on an upbeat note. I wondered if they had tested for powder burns before his finger-printing. And he'd probably washed his hands a million times since then. I remembered a few cases—not many—when the arresting officer neglected to Mirandize and the perp eventually walked on a tech.

"Elizabeth's a good lawyer. Everything will work out," I said again, trying to reassure myself as well.

I hung up and continued uptown. The heat of the day had dissipated and now Lenox Avenue was crowded. At 135th Street the cluster of vendors hawking their wares in the reflected light of Pan-Pan's restaurant was so busy it took me a minute to maneuver around the tables of scarves and socks and sunglasses.

City Hall had cleared them from 125th Street only to have some of the hardier souls regroup and resurface in the most unlikely places. Right now they were operating less than two blocks from the precinct.

Beyond the cluster of tables, I spotted Flyin' Home and his dogs moving down 135th Street toward the Kennedy Center basketball court. I called out and rushed after him, hoping he was in a better mood and more willing to talk about Friday night. But the dogs moved fast and by the time I reached the court no one was there.

By nine o'clock traffic was slow on the Harlem River. I stood on the terrace looking down into the water, wondering about Thea. How she had almost won the pageant . . . almost succeeded in becoming a great singer . . . almost found a good man. *Almost* had been the recurring theme in her life. What had happened along the way? How had she ended up working as a barmaid in the Half-Moon? Who had invited her into that alley?

"What're you thinking, Mali?"

Tad had stepped out onto the terrace and I turned at the sound of his voice. "Nothing much. Listening for the next boat. River's so quiet."

He moved close behind me and his hands found the place in the small of my back and slowly began to work their way down. He wore only a pair of shorts and his skin was wet and soft and had a just-bathed, warm, jasmine scent. I closed my eyes, forgetting about Thea.

"Muscles are a little tense, Baby . . ."

"So is yours," I whispered, leaning into him.

He kissed the nape of my neck, then lifted me and moved through the living room and into the bedroom. In the dim circle of light, he lay back on the bed watching me, smiling as I undressed.

"Ah, girl . . . the longer I know you, the better you look . . ." His voice was barely audible as I turned around, dropped my bra to the floor and stepped out of the silk bikini.

"And the longer I know you, the better you feel," I said.

"Come here," he whispered. "Baby, come here . . . walk slow . . . like that . . . that's it."

I stood near the edge of the bed, looking down, always surprised at the sight of him, surprised and glad at how fast he could get ready for action. He was ready and I hadn't even touched him. I stood there with my hands on my hips thinking of an old blues riff, wondering how Lettie would have worked it:

> . . . *Gimme a hot dog.*
> *For my roll.*
> *No mustard, may'naise.*
> *Oh my soul.*
> *Just that hot, hot dog.*
> *From my hot dog man . . .*

I was no singer, and to open my mouth to these words would have destroyed the mood, so I let the other parts of me do the talking. He reached for me with one hand and turned off the lamp with the other. "Tell me, Baby, what I want to hear."

I leaned over with my legs spread wide on either side of him. He moved down, and in the dark I felt his breath light and easy on my stomach.

Dawn was making its way over the edge of the river when I opened my eyes. Tugboat and barge horns sounded their hoarse notes, then faded off.

I listened for a minute to the smaller clatter of silverware and rose from the bed and wandered into the dining area near the terrace. The curtains blew with the soft scent of the river behind them. I looked at the table.

"Champagne and orange juice. Are we celebrating something?"

"Not a celebration," he said, stepping from the kitchen to place a platter of bacon and waffles on the table.

He was naked. How could a man stand at a stove with no clothes on? I watched him and my appetite stirred, but not for the waffles. He turned toward the stove again and I prayed that no hot oil would pop from the pan.

"I wanted to do something special," he said. "Something for you to remember while I'm away . . ."

"I have a lot to remember," I said, gazing at him. His skin was like Golden Blossom honey, only sweeter. At age forty, he had an edge of silver at his temples but prided himself for not having one slack muscle. I gazed at him another minute, then turned toward the bathroom to brush my teeth and dip my head in a rush of cold water. When I returned to the table, he was seated. I watched the other muscles move as he lifted his fork.

"How long will you be gone?"

"Two weeks or so."

It was the "or so" that got to me. I lifted my glass and did not offer a toast. In the middle of the night, when he had spoken of the training assignment in Los Angeles, I had rested my head on his chest, and for some unfathomable reason had begun to cry.

Maybe I hadn't wanted to hear bad news in the middle of something so good. Maybe there was such a thing as loving a person so much you ached to reach across even small distances to touch him.

And when I had finally slept, the dreams came: of the plane going down; of a South Central shoot-out and he hadn't worn his vest.

I had awakened shivering in sweat and had spent the next hour wrapped in his robe and kneeling on the terrace.

Somewhere out of the darkness I had felt a familiar presence, then heard something too slight and too soft to be a whisper. I knew who it was so I didn't turn around.

Don't worry about things before they happen, girl. Didn't I teach you anything? And get up off your knees if you're not praying . . .

No need to answer. I had remained quiet and gazed into the dark water until my mother's voice drifted off on the night breeze. My head cleared and I was able to creep back to bed.

Tad saw my expression now and reached across the table for my hand. "Come with me, Baby. Come on . . ."

I thought about it for a minute, pleased with the possibilities. I had entertained myself with vivid dreams of going away alone with him. Even if it was just across the street. I wanted to go. West Coast. West Nepal, west hell. Last summer in St. Croix, as nice as it had been after all the hell I'd been put through, didn't really count because the whole family had been there. Now here was the chance for just the two of us, and I had to shake my head.

As tolerant as Dad was of my lifestyle, he had grown old worrying about me. Now, as old as I was, I had to draw the line. This may have been the nineties but my wild ways had been a thorn in his side since I was sixteen. Now here I was, plucking out my own gray strands, and he still worried, still waited up. Mainly because Mom was gone and my sister, Benin, was also gone.

An occasional night out was one thing. Two weeks on the other side of the continent was quite another. If I went, I'd have to come back with a paper signed by a justice of the peace.

"Dad and Alvin would have a problem with that," I said, trying to explain in the shortest possible way. Even as I said it, I hurt. I felt worse when he whispered, "Ah. Well . . ." As if he understood something I didn't.

We finished breakfast in silence and I thought about crawling back into bed to divide the sections of the Sunday *Times,* but there was no time for reading. In the evening, he'd be gone.

We finished the champagne and I sat on the edge of the bed, fingering the tangled sheets and trying not to feel weepy, trying not to feel anything, and failing when he came close and I felt his mouth again, moving soft against my shoulder.

chapter seven

The main corridor in the Criminal Court Building was like Times Square at five o'clock and just as confusing if you didn't know where you were going. The pace was normal only at the check-in line, where bags were emptied of keys, guns, knives, tokens—anything metal. On the other side of the metal detector, chaos closed in, sweeping you into a parade of cops, clerks, attorneys, murderers, arsonists, and larcenists—grand and petty—and other visitors.

I walked fast, pulling Bertha by the hand. She pulled back to stare as several doors off the corridor swung open and closed on brief snapshots of other crises. Along the way we passed a young girl leaning against the wall with a crying baby. She was crying also, her round teenage face aged by incomprehensible circumstance. I imagined her man had probably been sentenced or denied bail or skipped bail and a warrant had been issued.

A few feet away, a middle-aged man was advising his probation officer: "If it wasn't for me, you wouldn't have a job." He sported a dirty Tommy Hilfinger sweatshirt and a scraggly red beard and was probably homeless, but what he said, he said grandly—as if he alone were propping up the entire criminal-justice apparatus.

I led Bertha onto a wide wing off the main corridor and we passed through a set of double doors into a small courtroom where Elizabeth was sitting in the first row, waiting for Kendrick to be brought in. I felt Bertha begin to shake. We managed to sit directly behind Elizabeth, and I tapped her shoulder. Bertha was silent and I did the talking. "When is Kendrick coming up?"

"Any minute."

"Ask him if he knows a woman, a white woman named Teddi Lovette, and how can I reach her. She came to Bertha's shop the day after Kendrick was arrested. I need to find her."

The door to the left of the judge's bench slid open and two officers accompanied Kendrick into the room. His face was hardrock handsome but he managed to smile and nod to us. Bertha's face was wet with tears and she passed a hand over her chest.

The judge cleared his throat and glanced at the court reporter. The prosecutor, a fat young man with thick lenses, rose from the table to the left and began to read from the indictment. Elizabeth and Kendrick and I already knew what it said, but in the prosecutor's mouth it sounded hard and cold and bloody. Words like *malice aforethought,* which would leave the ordinary defendant blinking and wondering who the hell Malice was.

Ain't had nuthin' to do with no Malice. He wasn't even on the scene.

". . . fatally wounded and thereby caused the death of one Thea Morris on the night of . . ."

I stopped listening and concentrated on Kendrick, on his well-shaped head and dark athlete's neck. He knew what malice was and did not bow his head but stared straight ahead, as if his vertebrae had been fused.

Finally: "How do you plead?"

The courtroom was small but appeared large in its emptiness. Except for five or six other people scattered along the sixteen rows of straight-backed wooden benches, there was nothing to absorb the echo. The court reporter glanced up to see if she had missed a nod or a frown, then resumed pressing the narrow keys on her machine. Sunshine filtered in thin and white through the high windows, discoloring the wooden rows.

"How do you plead?"

The question resonated from the old brass chandelier and the IN GOD WE TRUST sign on the wall above the bench.

"Not guilty!"

There was no echo in Kendrick's voice, only the hot dry anger of innocence. I looked down to see Bertha's fingers, like claws, etching the wood of the bench in front of us. A court officer stifled a yawn as Elizabeth rose from the table and began to speak: "Your Honor, my client's innocence will be proven. I request that he be released on bail until his trial date."

The judge did not glance up. I focused on his hair, on the thin silver strands spread strategically and ineffectually across his scalp. Patches of pink gleamed through and the sun caught them, sparkling with sweat, as he nodded. And I knew from the deliberate moves what was coming.

Judge Pink Patch cleared his throat. "At this time, the possibility exists that defendant, given the opportunity, may violate the terms and conditions of bail and not return to court at the appointed time. The court is aware that the defendant has a contract to work in Milan, Italy. The possibility exists that he may not return. Bail is therefore denied and trial is scheduled for Tuesday, October 1, 1997."

At first, I wondered where the sound was coming from: a low whimper that rose and settled like a high keen on the wind. Bertha's mouth was open and she had thrown her head back and crumpled into the seat, holding her hands to her chest. Kendrick, his eyes tearing, called to her. "Be strong, Bert. I'll be all right. Be strong."

At the sound of his voice, two officers attached themselves to each of his arms, as if they expected him to fly off through the barred windows, and a second later he disappeared through the door at the left of the bench.

Elizabeth had left the table and was bending over Bertha now, rubbing her hands, patting her shoulder.

"Listen, Bertha: This is not the last word. I'm going to keep trying for bail. After all, it isn't as if he's accused of shooting the president."

Outside, on Canal Street, the sun beat down like the fist of a seasoned heavyweight. Bertha walked like an old woman. Her face was streaked with tears and she was unusually quiet.

Suddenly, she stopped and stared at me. "How did that fuckin' judge know about that contract? I bet wasn't nobody but that funkpot Laws tipped them. Well, he gonna get what's comin' to him, you hear? He gonna get what's comin'. Mark my words."

We threaded our way through the maze of electronics and seafood stalls cluttering the sidewalk, and I wondered why the vendors had been pushed from 125th Street while this street had been left untouched. The thought lasted only a second because Bertha's voice was rising again, bubbling up like yeast in the dry afternoon heat.

"I bet it was Laws sent a letter. He was jealous of Kendrick, that's what. He knew if Kendrick went to Italy, he wasn't comin' back to no damn small-time bar. His life woulda been changed. His career woulda taken off . . . his actin' and everything . . ."

I nodded and glanced at her as we headed for the subway, wondering if those were Kendrick's plans or the dreams that she herself had for him. I listened and thought again of Kendrick standing before the court, straight and silent, and the judge never looking up. I thought of Alvin. He was going to call this evening. My attention veered away and I no longer heard Bertha. I was busy fashioning a lie for Alvin.

chapter eight

I fixed Bertha a pot of Sleepy Time herbal tea, made sure she was comfortable, then I back-tracked downtown. Forty-second Street was more crowded than ever now that the Disney renaissance had replaced all the ratty peep shows, adult bookshops, and porn theaters.

Two blocks west, on Ninth Avenue, a high-rise apartment complex for performing artists stood surrounded by new soft-lit restaurants where regular hamburgers now masqueraded as minced New York sirloin on fresh sesame bun, coffee had names with accents, and menus were slid under your nose by wait staff who'd scored high on the Madison Avenue-boutique test for attitude.

I found the place I was looking for tucked away on the third floor in one of a string of small buildings known as Theater Row, across from the high-rise complex. In the small lobby, I picked up a flyer and history of the company before climbing a narrow stairway to a door spray-painted with the company's name, Star Manhattan.

It was a small space, no more than sixty seats, and a rehearsal was in progress, so I eased into a seat three rows from the last. According to the history, seven actors worked in repertory on the weekends—six since Kendrick was in jail, but his name was still on the flyer and his handsome face still smiled from the company's roster.

Four of the six sat in the first row watching Teddi Lovette onstage, crouched in front of an older woman seated on a tattered brown velvet sofa. The woman looked straight ahead, staring into the space that the audience occupied on weekends.

Teddi bowed her head and held tightly to the woman's arm. Then she broke off in midsentence and quickly got to her feet.

"This isn't working, guys. Doesn't feel right just yet. There's a certain . . ."

Behind me, a sliver of light stabbed the darkness. Someone, a woman who had been sitting in the last row, got up and left. No one in the first row turned around, but concentrated on Teddi Lovette as she paced the stage, moving like a cat in her black leotard and print wrap skirt. Onstage, she appeared taller than I remembered. She squeezed her eyes shut and pushed her hair into a tight ball, back from her face—a gesture vaguely familiar, though I couldn't remember where I'd seen it. Finally she sighed. "Okay, that's it for today.

We've been working hard since this morning. This was good but we can make it better by Friday, okay?"

Nods and murmurs as the group, three men and two women, rose and gathered their things. The network of klieg lights criss-crossing the ceiling blinked once and the stage went dark. In the dim glow of ordinary lighting, the group filed past me and I caught the low murmur.

"Where're we eating?" the woman who had been onstage asked.

"Billy's, I guess."

"Yeah. Kendrick's not home and—"

"Damn, he got a bad break . . ."

They glanced at me and nodded as they filed past. I waved and smiled quickly as I made my way down front and across the small stage to the back, where Teddi had disappeared. I didn't know if there was another exit and I wasn't taking any chances. She hadn't returned my calls and it was time to find out why.

The dressing room was not a dressing room in the strict sense: no star on the door because there was no door, only a space cleared in a corner for three small tables with makeup mirrors and unshaded lamps, a half dozen folding chairs stacked near two coat-racks hung with costumes, and a large steamer trunk stuffed with wigs, gloves, hats, and other accessories. Coils of electrical cable ringed the area like thick snakes, and I trod over them carefully. I was a foot away when Teddi leaned close to the mirror, then turned to face me. "Hi?"

It was a question more than a greeting, which

meant she didn't remember me. "I'm Mali Anderson," I answered, "a friend of Kendrick's sister. I've been trying to contact you—"

"Oh." Her face brightened at the mention of Kendrick. "Come in. Come in."

I looked around and stepped across the imaginary boundary that defined the perimeter of the dressing area. She closed the lid of the trunk and waved her hand.

"Here. Have a seat. I apologize for not returning your calls. I . . ." She spread her hands wide. "I've been so . . ."

I eased down onto the trunk but couldn't get comfortable. A part of an old-fashioned hand fan was sticking out and scratching my thigh when I moved. I smiled anyway. "That's all right. I know how it is. I only caught part of the rehearsal, but what I saw, I liked. Kendrick talked about the group all the time and I'm glad I finally got a chance to see you folks."

I said this with what I hoped was a straight face. Kendrick had never mentioned a thing to me until today in court, when he'd given Elizabeth the company's address. I wondered if he'd even mentioned it to Alvin. Probably not. This was a small group and perhaps he was waiting for a part in a larger production before inviting friends and family. I thought of asking Alvin, but that might lead to other, more complicated, questions.

Teddi had been brushing her hair when I'd approached and now she placed the brush on the table near a wig stand.

"How's he doing?"

"As well as can be expected, I guess. The judge refused bail."

"Oh, God." She closed her eyes and touched her hair with her fingers, and there was that oddly familiar gesture again. "Everyone's just devastated over this. We . . . miss him so much. We can't understand how this could have happened." Her eyes shone and she blinked rapidly. "What's going to happen? He didn't do it. He's not like that. He told me himself that they were just friends."

I gazed at her and right away translated all those plurals—we miss him, we can't understand, *we*—to a single voice. Her voice.

"How long have you known him?"

She rested her elbows against the cluttered table, busily calculating a time and date she probably had already encoded in a special place. Finally, she sighed. "About three months, since he joined the group. We hit it off right away."

We hit it off right away.

I wanted to smile. Thank God for melanin in colored folks. We can lie and if we don't get too shifty-eyed can get away with a truckload of bullshit. Other folks, on the other hand, had a serious problem when the red started creeping across their cheekbones. As was happening now with Teddi. It's damn hard to hide the fever of love.

We hit it off right away hung in the air until I said, "The rest of the crew is gone. I'm not holding you up, am I?"

"No. Not at all. I'm meeting someone else. My mother. But I have time."

"So how is Kendrick—as an actor? Is he good?"

Some of the tightness left her face, and when she smiled, her teeth were bright and slightly crooked. Her voice was softer, quite different from the stage voice. "He's very good." The tone made me wonder if she was describing his talent on- or offstage.

"Well," I said, "too bad he may have to spend hard time in jail for something he didn't do."

The smile disappeared and she leaned forward, closing the space between us. "Listen: How well did you know Thea?" Her voice had dropped to a whisper, although I was sure there was no one else on the floor but the two of us.

"Well, I knew her but we weren't what you'd call close friends," I whispered.

"Did you know any of her family? Her mother, father, grandmother?" She spoke as if she was running out of time.

"No, I—"

"That's what I need to know."

"Why?"

"Because . . . I . . . we all know how and when and where she died. But if I can find out *why* she died, it might lead to . . . whoever wanted her out of their way. Maybe something or someone in—"

We both heard the quiet tap of high heels across the stage, and I watched Teddi's face. A mask of chalk, stiff and formal, slid in place as she rose from her seat and walked to the edge of the boundary with outstretched arms. "Watch your step, Mother. You can trip up in here."

A voice came out of the darkness, soft but impatient. "Trip up? I've been waiting downstairs for the past twenty minutes. I—"

The woman who had slipped out of the door while Teddi was onstage had come back. She stopped abruptly when she saw me and her expression tore through an impressive number of changes in record time—surprise, fright, wariness, before finally settling into a tight smile. All this while stepping forward to shake my hand as Teddi introduced me.

Mrs. Lovette was about fifty years old, give or take a year or two, Miami-tanned, and slim, with silver blond hair pulled up to tighten the skin around the large, well-made-up eyes. Her white linen suit was fashionably wrinkled and the tiny black patent bag swinging from her shoulder was only wide enough to accommodate lip blush, eyeliner, and two major credit cards.

Her nose was narrowed as if she'd just strolled past a cosmetic counter and some clerk had wafted a stream of cheap perfume at her, but the tight smile held. Between mother and daughter, the mother so far was the Academy Award contender.

I remained silent, listening as Teddi outdid herself spinning a story: "Mali's interested in joining the group."

"Indeed. Well, it will be a pleasure to see you onstage. Have you any experience in acting?"

All my life, I wanted to say, wondering what the

hell was going on. I nodded and said, "Nothing much. Church plays and things like that. Nothing much."

Her smile grew smaller. "Do you live uptown? Harlem?"

"Well, I—"

"She lives in Brooklyn, Mother," Teddi cut in. "Why do you think all black people live in Harlem? She lives in Brooklyn." And with a shake of her head, added, "Bed-Stuy, right?"

I stared at her. The girl had moved me from Harlem to Brooklyn in a blink.

"Right," I finally said, waiting to see what would happen next. Mrs. Lovette remained silent as Teddi turned to me. "I'll get back to you in a few days. I'm sure it'll be good news."

She was rushing now, throwing things into her straw bag and moving in the small space to turn off the lamps on the dressing tables. This left us in semidarkness and I was glad because no amount of melanin could hide the confusion on my face.

As we stepped off the stage and moved up the narrow aisle toward the door, Teddi was still talking—trying to get everything out and let nothing in. I was bringing up the rear, and she turned to me and said, "Mother's on the board of several foundations, a few of which underwrite our productions quite generously."

We reached the street and I said, "Nice to meet you, Mrs. Lovette."

Her reply was dry and polite, as if she hadn't recovered from the shock of meeting me. Then she moved to the curb, where a limo was waiting. Teddi paused and fumbled in her bag, searching for something. I waited.

"Listen," she said, her head still down. "There's something I need to know. Very badly. But don't call me. I will call you tomorrow. I promise. I will."

Then she looked up, smiling toward the car. "I've got to go now," she whispered through teeth that barely seemed to move, like a ventriloquist prompting a dummy. Then aloud, "You'll definitely hear from me."

She climbed into the car, and I watched it pull away from the curb.

I was lying across the bed dreaming of Tad when Alvin phoned. He came on the line sounding at least an octave lower than when he'd last called, and I wondered if he'd already started to sprout chest hair in the two weeks he'd been away. He was only twelve years old, but with his new basso-profundo sound could easily sub for Isaac Hayes on WRKS.

"What's up, Mali?"

"Nothing much. What's up with you?"

With a voice like that, I decided not to tease him with my usual "How're the girls" question, preferring at this point not to know. When he returned home there would be time enough to deal with the necessary questions of sex and puberty and male hormones. Right now, I stayed on neutral ground. "How's fishing?" I asked.

"Great. I caught a lot of fish, but the other day I got stung by some jellyfish."

I wondered if I should be alarmed. Jellyfish. Last summer he had talked about a sea creature called man-o-war that sounded like some battleship equipped to blow a hole through a fortress. Before I could ask, he went on: "It's a clear blob but it holds a poison that can paralyze—"

"Oh, God! Alvin, are you all right? When did this happen?"

"Aw, Mali. It was a few days ago. I'm fine. Captain Bo and another fisherman pulled me out of the water and packed hot sand on my back and arms. The sand drew out the poison. I'm fine. It didn't even leave any marks. You'll see when I get home."

"You're sure you're okay?"

"I'm okay. I guess I shouldn't've told you 'cause you worry so much."

"I can't help it, Alvin. I love you."

"Aw, Mali, I know. I know. Listen, lemme speak to Grandpa."

"He's at the club. Has a gig three nights a week now and loving every minute of it."

"Man, that's everything. Well, tell him hello, and Mali?"

"Yes?"

"Please don't tell him about the jellyfish thing. He worries more than you do, except he doesn't show it."

"Okay, I—"

"Captain Bo's calling me. Gotta go."

"Be careful, Alvin."

"I'll call again, maybe tomorrow."

He hung up. For the next few minutes, when I drew my breath, my chest hurt. He had not asked about Kendrick. Maybe tomorrow he will. Time enough for me to ask about the repertory group.

chapter nine

The house of detention loomed large on Centre Street in downtown Manhattan. Some folks said that the newer building a block north of the older Gothic structure was nicer, with its dorm-style details. I could see no difference between the old and the new.

In the visitors' area, Bertha and I were searched, scanned with the metal detector, and given a number. An hour later we were led into the visiting area and seated at a long table separated by a wire-mesh screen. The seats were divided among cubicles.

Kendrick was brought in wearing a nondescript uniform of heavy gray cotton and rubber shoes. The uniform had no pockets and he wore no socks.

A faint gray discoloration appeared to have seeped into his chocolate skin tone and his eyes—deep-set and normally dreamy—now seemed to shift between list-lessness and wariness. He sat down and smiled and pressed his hand against the mesh barrier, and Bertha pressed her palm against his.

"How they treatin' you, Kendrick?"

He shrugged and smiled, knowing there was nothing she could do about whatever went on behind the closed doors of cells.

"Okay. I don't mess with nobody and nobody messes with me. They got some games people play in here, but my black belt let them know I'm not down with that program . . ."

"Elizabeth's still trying for bail," I said, knowing how important it was to leave him something to hold on to after we were gone. "She's still trying."

"Yeah. I know she is. She's one smart sister. I like her."

Then he pressed his hands to his face and rubbed his eyes. "I don't know, Mali. I don't know. It's hard to even guess what's gonna happen from one day to the next. All I do is try to watch my back, and don't walk away from a fight. If you walk away in here, you're done. For some guys, there's no difference between night and day. Both are bad. For me, the nights are worse. As soon as my head hits the bed, the nightmares come on. Real bad ones. Thea's head is in my lap and I'm tryin' to push that stuff back inside her. I see her face and I'm tryin' to tell her I didn't mean it."

"Didn't mean what?" I asked.

He looked at me and I thought he was about to break, but he drew a deep breath and blinked until the moment passed and he was able to continue.

"Earlier that night, Thea and I had had a few

words. I wanted to start . . . start seeing her again, you know. But . . . she shrugged and said it was too late, that she was pregnant. She was gonna have a kid. She was three months along. I heard that and I kinda lost it, I guess. Called her every name I could think of. Whore, prostitute. Said one man's dick hadn't cooled off before she was on another. Selling herself to the heaviest wallet.

"I was so mad I wanted to hurt her, to knock her down. But I didn't. I could never've done that."

"What did you do?"

"I called Bert and talked to her, asked her to come to the bar."

"But you didn't tell me she was . . . ," Bert began.

"I know, I know. Maybe because I didn't want to believe it myself. I should've taken that night off. Just chilled. But it was her birthday. I wanted to hang in just to see who gave her the biggest present, then I'd know for sure who the guy was. I mean, I had some idea, but the way it turned out . . . By then, it was too late to take back my words, to tell her I didn't mean what I'd said.

"I loved her, and she died believing that I thought she was a whore. In my dream, I'm tryin' to tell her, but her face is gone. She can't hear me. The only sound is those dogs howling . . ."

"Dogs?"

"Yeah. Like big dogs, howling right over my shoulder."

"I heard them dogs myself," Bertha added. "That

ain't your imagination. You ain't goin' crazy. I heard them myself. First they was barkin'. Then a few minutes later they set up a howl."

She turned to me, surprised. "I don't know how I coulda forgot to mention that, Mali."

"I know who those dogs were," I said. "Flyin' Home owns those dogs. He was out there. He told me so."

They looked at me as if I had delivered the key that would've allowed Kendrick to walk.

"I'll speak to Lieutenant Honeywell," I said. "Maybe he can bring Flyin' Home into the precinct house for questioning. Maybe he saw something.

"Listen, Kendrick: Maybe this has nothing to do with anything, but if you still cared for Thea and were trying to get back with her, where does Teddi fit in? Or should I be asking?"

He shook his head and smiled. "No, it's all right. I met her when I auditioned, about three months ago. Has enough dollars to buy half of Broadway if she wanted to. We had a drink one night after rehearsal but nothing else happened. I was still thinking about Thea, hoping things could've worked out. Teddi and I are friends, that's all."

Two hours in this room flew by faster than two minutes, and before we knew it the guard was standing in back of Kendrick, tapping him on the shoulder. He looked up, then back at us, and raised his right fist.

"Be strong, Bert. Things gonna work out." He smiled, a deep, heartbreaking, genuine smile this time, and was gone.

Bertha and I rode the elevator down in silence. At least she hadn't cried or cursed or done any of the things I'd expected, given her short temper. But once outside, she grabbed my arm.

"Listen. When you gonna speak to Honeywell? How soon?"

"He's out of town. I expect him back in ten days. Meanwhile, I'm going to look for Flyin' Home myself. We go back a ways. He doesn't actually owe me anything, but he'll remember how I treated him when he was brought into the precinct house all those times. Maybe he'll remember me calling him *mister* when some of the other law-and-order officers were tripping over their tongues calling him *nigger*. And maybe he'll remember me telling him, after his accident, about SSI and the rehab institute."

We moved toward the subway and waited on the platform for the IRT. I turned to Bertha as the train roared into the station. Above the noise, I said, "Maybe he will, Bertha, and maybe he won't. That's all I can tell you about him. But one way or the other, with or without him, we're going to get Kendrick out."

We boarded the train and rode up to 135th Street and Lenox Avenue. I glanced at her from time to time, thinking she had fallen asleep. She was awake, staring at the vacant blond in the Guess-jeans advertisement. Finally she said, "Thea was pregnant. Can you imagine that?"

"No," I said. "I can't."

chapter ten

On Thursday, Dad and I attended Thea's funeral, three days after Kendrick was arraigned. Teddi still had not called. It was so crowded at the funeral parlor that half the visitors were milling around outside in the street. But despite the confusion, someone spotted Dad who knew that Thea had sung with his band, and she escorted us in.

The narrow aisles were clogged and row after row was packed. More than one face had makeup melting, and I knew that if this service lasted too long, tempers would start to rise. Dad's temperature had risen earlier when he objected to my outfit—the only black dress I owned, a sleeveless silk with a hemline hovering, he complained, just below my navel. "We're going to a funeral, not a fashion show!"

"I have nothing else to wear, and I intend to be comfortable," I said. The standoff had lasted almost a half hour and I had wondered if we'd make the service at all. Finally I compromised and offered to bring a shawl to spread over my knees when I sat down. I also added a cluster of black silk roses to the brim of my yellow straw hat and pulled on an old pair of Mom's crocheted yellow gloves. This seemed to calm him enough for us to leave the house.

Now the heat closed in and I tried to concentrate on the banks of flowers surrounding the closed casket. Gladys sat in the first row, shoulders rigid, looking neither to the left nor the right.

A young reverend who probably hadn't known Thea did the best he could under the circumstances and managed to deliver an impassioned eulogy, concentrating on her talent, her ambition, and the tragedy of her death. Then a tall, straight-backed woman wearing a wide pale blue straw hat walked to the front and without introduction began to sing "Amazing Grace."

Her voice, like a tide washing over grains of sand, lifted and carried us away.

I glanced at Dad and then put my arm around him. Sometimes, people attending the same service, and sitting in the same room, cry for different reasons. I didn't know if he was mourning Thea or the memory of Mom and Benin. Or mourning all those dreams we never quite catch up to.

The last notes drifted and the singer moved away and then someone was speaking, focusing again on Thea's talent. I heard Dad's name called, saw him get up and walk to the front. His words drifted away from me as I closed my eyes and thought of the seriously emotional send-offs that black folks are known for. We

whoop and we holler to send the spirit on its way, make
noise so it wouldn't want to come back. But there was
no falling-down-screaming testimony today.

Then Gladys was talking, every pleat and fold of
her black silk suit carved in place, like her expression.
She spoke of the Thea she had known a dozen years
ago—the model and the beauty.

But there was no substance to the reminiscence
and I wondered how close they had really been. Then
again, they had probably been only as close as Thea had
allowed.

Gladys's voice rose in tears when the tall straight-
backed woman came forward once more to sing, and
again when a slim brown man of about forty, handsome
in a pinstriped suit, approached the casket, rested his
hand on the side, then turned and walked out.

And to my surprise, he was followed by Teddi
Lovette, looking almost Victorian in deep black, down
to her stockings. She also touched the casket, running
her pale fingers lightly against the mahogany wood.
Even her fingernails were painted black. She turned
quickly and left.

I wanted to follow her, to ask why she was there,
and why she hadn't called me as she'd promised. I
needed to know more than that, but if I had moved
Dad would've reached out and probably nailed me to
my seat.

I glanced at my watch and then at the program. It
had taken less than an hour and less than a page to sum
up Thea's talent and beauty. What about her life? The
one-paragraph obituary only mentioned the date of

birth and where she had gone to school. The Miss New York State pageant information took five lines of the paragraph, but there was not one line about her surviving relatives. What was going on? I thought about what Gladys had said: Perhaps Thea had indeed been dropped here from another planet.

We filed out into a relatively cool eighty degrees, and some of the pinched faces smoothed out. I scanned the crowd but Teddi was nowhere in sight. Why had she shown up with so much black on? Since she had been the only white person at the funeral, she couldn't have blended in no matter what she'd worn.

Most of the mourners were the ones I had seen crowded into the Half-Moon for the wake. Now they gathered like flamboyant peacocks, shaking their ruffled feathers in the noon brightness.

I watched this parade of spandex and gold and wondered how Dad could've been so upset about my dress. As brief as it was, at least it was a respectable black.

I walked to the curb to stand near the tall woman with the voice. She had chestnut-tinted braids under the brim that softened her face, so it was difficult to estimate her age. She glanced at me and smiled as the crowd moved around us. People piled into cars and edged away, glad for the artifical comfort of the air-conditioning.

Dad appeared much more composed now and moved through the crowd, shaking hands and waving as if he were running for office. At sixty-two, with smooth gray hair cut close against his chocolate face, he was an attractive man. He approached, smiling at the woman standing beside me.

"Miss Adele. Your pipes are as cool and you're as beautiful as ever."

She reached out to touch his shoulder. "Where you get off with this *Miss* Adele stuff, Sweetie? That ain't what you used to call me back when."

Her voice was wonderful and deep and she hugged Dad, laughing good-naturedly.

"This is Mali, my daughter," Dad said. "Last time you saw her, she was in knee-highs."

She turned to me, still laughing. "And look at the lady now. Legs long enough to cause a serious traffic jam. How're you doing, Sweetie? And you have those pale gray eyes, just like your mama had. I remember when she toured with Katherine Dunham. You a dancer? God knows those legs were meant for more than walkin'."

I smiled and extended my hand. This was Miss Adele. Gladys had said she was seventy-something but she looked at least twenty years younger. Miss Adele had been Thea's voice coach, the lady I needed to talk to.

"Thea pulled quite a crowd," Dad said, shading his eyes against the white sun.

"And half of them probably didn't even know her," Miss Adele said. "Probably came just for the show."

We watched the last of the lingerers kiss, wave, and move on to the other business of the day. "The only thing I can say about all of this," she sighed, "is Dessie can rest in peace."

"Amen to that. But listen, Adele: We gotta keep in touch. Ain't many old folks like us left. We gotta stay connected."

"Jeffrey, my door is always open. I'd love to see you other than at somebody's funeral."

With that, she kissed his cheek and stepped out into the street. Dad held open the door of the cab and waved as she pulled away.

Dad was quiet as we walked the short distance home. Finally I asked, "Who's Dessie?"

"Dessie Hamilton. Barmaid back in the day who worked in the Half-Moon. So popular that the place was supposed to close for a week when she died. Folks in the know said she'd been the world's oldest living barmaid till one night she strolled to Harlem Hospital in her famous five-inch heels, complaining of a bad stomach, but it was a bad liver kept her there, and days later took her away.

"At her age, she deserved the honor of a bar closing, but rumor had it that the owner of the place—who everybody called Dandy Dan when he paid off on the numbers and Goddamn Dan when he didn't—used the occasion of her passing to realize a dream of his own.

"When she died, Goddamn Dan closed the bar and stepped off the earth. Ain't been seen or heard from since. Later, we found that he'd stepped with a quarter million in numbers receipts—big, big dollars in those days.

"Now rumor also had it that if a place reopened

with new management but didn't 'clean the four corners,' nothing but bad luck would come of it. Half-Moon reopened ten years ago, and for the next few years must've broken the record for bad luck. So many shoot-outs, knife fights, and thrown lye that the place was known as the Body-of-the-Month Club. Stuff like that kept the sensible folks away. Then the owner, who nobody ever saw anyway, wised up and walked.

"Then Henderson Laws came in with new dollars and new decor but was too cheap to pay the spiritualist man who had 'cleaned' the four corners with a special water one hour before the grand opening. Instead, he pushed a fifth of bottom-shelf gin on him. Well, you know how that goes. Everybody in the know kept quiet, and kinda waited."

"Why was Thea working there when she could've done so much better? I mean, with her talent and her sophistication, why would she settle for that place?"

"Who knows . . ."

We turned into 139th Street between Seventh and Eighth Avenues and reconnected with the ordinary rhythm of our lives. We waved across the street to a neighbor who was trimming her hedges, and to another who was walking his dog.

Inside, Dad picked up Ruffin's leash. "Back in a little while." He waved to me, and I watched him leave the house with the dog at his side. He was upset and wanted to be alone. I'd ask about Dessie, the old barmaid, and her connection to Thea, later.

chapter eleven

hen Dad returned home, I held up Dr. Thomas's invitation from among the three piles of mail divided into "important," "not-so," and "discard." The letter had a two-week-old postmark.

"Dad, why is this at the bottom of the 'not-so' pile? Aren't you going?"

"Of course I am and I already told him so. The invite's only a formality. I didn't mention it because I didn't think you'd be interested in another boring social—'B.S. gathering,' as you called them."

"I want to go to this one," I said, surprising him. He had taken off his jacket and was helping to sort the rest of the mail, even though he was paying me to do that.

"You know, Mali, I can't understand you sometimes. Three years ago, I had to practically drag you to the affair. This time, you can't wait to get there."

He rose from the table and headed for the window. "Let me see if there's a full moon or something . . ."

"Very funny. I said I'd go and you get all—"

"Well, I know how you feel about Michaels. Your nose gets narrow if I mention his name."

"And I still don't like him. But since Blaine Thomas expects a major musical contribution from you, I may as well enjoy a major meal."

I slit open the envelope and read the silver-edged card.

THE COMMITTEE TO REELECT EDWIN MICHAELS
REQUESTS YOUR PRESENCE AT
A FUND-RAISING DINNER
AT THE HOME OF DR. AND MRS. BLAINE THOMAS
WEDNESDAY, JULY 23

I read further, noting Dad's name on the bottom, just under the address.

Dr. Thomas lived two doors away with his wife and twin sons in a three-story limestone. Their double parlor was large enough to accommodate at least one hundred guests, and the rear garden, though overgrown with rose of Sharon and a spreading bed of ivy around an old bronze fountain, could probably hold twenty or so more.

Each guest was expected to pledge a minimum of five hundred dollars for the privilege of calling Senator Michaels by his first name for a few hours. More out of friendship with Dr. Thomas than as a contribution, Dad had offered to sit at the piano for a few hours.

This crowd, depending on to whom you spoke, made up the movers and shakers of Harlem, so I didn't expect to come away with any information about Thea. But I needed to observe Michaels, see how he was holding up in the face of his loss. He hadn't shown up for the funeral, and on one of the local talk shows he had seemed subdued and distracted. On television, the lines at the corners of his mouth were so deep that no amount of makeup could hide them.

I folded the card back into the envelope. It wasn't the meal that interested me. Dad said that the cops had moved too fast when they'd arrested Kendrick. I needed to be in the same room with Michaels again, to watch his moves up close.

The next day, Friday, dawned gray and drizzly, and I had slept badly. Tad had called at 2 A.M. and his voice, loving and soothing, still could not soften the fact that he was being held over in Los Angeles an additional week. I listened, nodding my head as if he were sitting next to me on the bed.

When he hung up, I clicked on WRKS-FM and sat by the window, staring out on the empty street, waiting patiently for the sounds of Billy Ocean to dissolve the numb feeling that had inched its way into my stomach. I gave up at 4:30 and stepped into the shower.

An hour later, a cup of Dad's Jamaican Blue Mountain coffee made me feel more human, better able to open my mouth without howling. I picked up Ruffin's leash, and we stepped out into the deserted street.

The dawn spreading over the street by inches dissolved some of the mist but patches of gray remained. We strolled down 135th Street between Seventh and Eighth Avenues where the tinge of pale, early sunlight delineated the row of star-shaped plaques embedded in the pavement—testaments to folks who had impacted the lives and culture of African-Americans: Malcolm X; Tito Puente; Percy Sutton. The bronze-edged stars continued for half a block: David Dinkins, Lois Alexander, Hope Stevens, Arturo Schomburg, Ella Fitzgerald.

Alvin had made a point of going to the Research Center to write a bio on each of these people.

In the quiet, the pad of Ruffin's paws tipped lightly as we retraced our steps and strolled past St. Mark's Church on Edgecombe Avenue. The sun was up now and splashing orange against the stained-glass windows. I thought about Kendrick's nightmares. And Bertha remembering not only the howling but the ordinary barking. How near had Flyin' Home been to the alley?

Back on Eighth Avenue and a few blocks south, I walked through a small scattering of street people. Some of the homeless—men, women, and children together in a tight phalanx—moved slowly, steering broken shopping carts crammed with the pitiful detritus of their shattered lives. Some others, wiry young men, moved faster than most nine-to-fivers and I recognized the nervous tic, the need to connect with the next hit. Their eyes, old and fever-bright, scanned me and slid away at the sight of Ruffin.

At 133rd Street I heard the whine of wheels before Flyin' Home turned the corner onto Eighth Avenue. A click sound through his teeth halted the dogs. They seemed more polite this time and sat without a bark. I reined in Ruffin anyway.

"How you doin', Mali? You out early again."

"Ruffin needs his exercise and so do I," I said. "How're you doing?"

He brought his hand up and tipped his cap forward, shading his eyes. Sweat had already stained the T-shirt under his powerful arms. "I'm a finish my business and head right back to the crib. Things ain't too cool 'round here lately."

"Like what?"

"Like at the Half-Moon, that's what."

"That's what I wanted to ask you about, Flyin'. I need to know if—"

He jerked his head back as if I'd slapped him. Then he pulled his chair back. "Naw, Mali. I don't know nuthin'. I don't know shit this time."

I heard the sharp snap sound of his teeth and once again he was gone before I could ask what in the world he meant.

When I walked in, Dad was at the table with a cup of coffee, thumbing through the *Daily Challenge*.

"Heard the news?"

"No. What happened?"

"Look at this," he said, pushing the paper toward me. "Damn joint still jinxed."

I looked at the headline, then sat down quickly to read.

Bad luck, like a bolt of lightning, struck again as death visited the Half-Moon for the second time. Henderson Laws, the fifty-eight-year-old owner and manager of the popular watering hole, was murdered last night, a little more than one week after his barmaid, Thea Morris, a former New York State beauty finalist, was fatally shot. Laws was discovered at 5 A.M. when the night porter arrived to clean the premises. The body, with a dozen stab wounds to the neck and back, was found lying facedown on the floor of his rear office. No money had been taken. There were no signs of forced entry, but police believe Laws had interrupted a robbery and the thief panicked, fleeing empty-handed after the killing. The weapon was not recovered.

So this was what Flyin' Home had meant.

I looked at Dad sipping his coffee and before I could frame the question he put his cup down and said, "Well, they can't pin that one on Kendrick, can they?"

I moved from the table, taking the paper with me. A robbery. And so many wounds, most of them in the back. Why was he at the bar at that late hour? No sign of forced entry. It had to be someone he knew.

•   •   •

Bertha had a full house when I walked into the shop. It was noon, time enough for this latest news to have circulated as far as it needed to go.

A thin teenager with smooth copper skin was in the chair having a finger wave, and another, older girl of about twenty or so sat under the dryer. Next to her, a heavy-set vanilla-faced woman of about thirty sat sipping coffee and thumbing through a back issue of *Black Hair.* I could have told her to put the magazine away because in the end Bert would decide what was best and change the woman's mind in less time than it took to pop the cap on a bottle of Dark and Lovely.

Bert looked up when I walked in. "Well, I see that lyin' ass got what was comin'. Bodies fallin' like flies, but they can't blame it on Kendrick this time. Need to be careful what we do 'cause shit got a way of rollin' back."

I let that go for the moment and made my way to the coffee-maker. I returned with a steaming cup and took a seat next to the woman with the magazine. The younger girl on the other side appeared to be dozing despite the noise from the dryer.

Bert said no more and I sipped the coffee and looked around the small shop. The TV was not on and the hum of the hair dryer was almost pleasant.

As often as I came here, I was still fascinated by the pictures of the assorted hairstyles Bert had pasted on the walls. Faces young and pretty enough to pass muster even if they were bald, but there they were, smiling from the circular cutouts, with hair blond, strawberry, auburn, and black; streaked, straightened, slicked, puffed, curled, crunched, waved, permed, relaxed, leisured, woven, wigged, glued, bleached, and braided. Smiling a promise of a better image that naturally translated into a vision of a better job, better man, and endless nights of knockout sex—though I wondered how much sex could be on the menu without disturbing the elaborate waves and curls framing some of the faces.

But hope, being what it is, brought them through the door to settle themselves in the chair and point to a picture and declare, "That's me."

Sometimes Bert suggested an alternative. Sometimes she didn't and nodded and smiled and went on with the alternative anyway. So skillfully, in fact, that in the end, the satisfied sister doubled the tip.

For a while—a short while—Bert had had Thea's picture pasted among the cutouts. But after Thea and Kendrick split up, Bert had removed it without a word.

I watched her hands now, moving over her customer's head, shaping each wave.

"What goes around, comes around," she said.

The woman sitting next to me closed the *Black Hair* magazine and said, "They shoulda named that place the Bad-Luck Bar for all the strange shit that went down in there . . . I'm talkin' grimy stuff!"

"Like what?" I asked.

She shrugged and looked at me as though I were a visitor from out of town. "That used to be my chill spot once upon a time, but like I said, some funny stuff was happenin' . . ."

"Like what?" I asked again.

She raised her cup to her mouth, trying to make

up her mind whether I was friend or foe. Bert said nothing and continued to style the girl's hair. The hum of the dryer competed with the drone of the air conditioner over the door. Outside, a jeep with stadium-size speakers pulled up to the traffic light. A sonic boom passed through the shop and the coffee cup vibrated in my hand. The light changed, the jeep's presence faded, and the electronic drones dominated again.

Finally, the woman yawned, and the chance to be the first with the news got the better of her. She leaned forward and her voice, like an invisible hand, drew us into an imperceptible circle.

"Everybody knows that place, but not everybody knows how Henderson Laws is. Was. I had a cousin we used to call Wild Thing. Young boy, pretty, and lived down to his name. Ended up HIV and went out on the A-train three months ago.

"Last summer, he spotted me in the Moon and pulled my coat. Said, 'Girlfriend, ain't no need chillin' here. If you ain't got no lollipop need workin', you wastin' your good time . . .'

"And you know, for the longest time I hadn't been able to figure why I couldn't get not one a those brothers to say hello, let alone buy me a glass of water. But once Wild Thing hipped me to the program, I peeped what was goin' down. I mean it wasn't exactly an out-'n'-out scene, you know what I'm sayin'. There was a lotta other folks droppin' in, but Laws kinda set the tone, you know . . . so I stopped hangin', 'cause I couldn't see past them undercover lovers he had strollin' in. . . ."

I looked at Bertha in the mirror, watched her bland expression as she continued to frame the face of the young woman in the chair. She glanced up and saw me watching, but her expression did not change and her hands did not stop moving. So far, she had not said a word.

"My cousin was part of that stroll," the woman continued, rolling up the magazine and tapping her palm. "And I know for a fact that a lot more gonna come out before all is said and done. I mean, talk had it that Laws was workin' it when he went."

"Who said?"

"Street said." She smiled, putting the magazine down and picking up the coffee cup again. It had to be cold by now but she sipped anyway, mostly for effect, I thought. "Street said," she repeated.

It was like the end of debating a point in religion or politics when someone declares, "The Bible said," or "The Constitution said." In some circles, "Street said" carried the same weight.

When no one broke the silence, I finally spoke: "I heard Laws was married."

She rolled her eyes as if that were the joke of the year: "Coupla times. Had an assembly line, three of which he managed to lend his name to at one time or other. But everybody knows he was pullin' shade."

"He was frontin'?"

"Frontin' and backin' and everything else, and as an extra bonus he was knockin' his star barmaid . . ."

"Thea?"

"That's the one. But through it all, he loved that

other stuff too. Seem like he couldn't pass up nothin' with a hole in it. Too bad he didn't stick to doughnuts."

At the mention of Thea's name, Bert's hand froze, then a second later resumed combing the girl's hair.

"Looks is deceivin'," Bert said quietly. "Looks is damn sure deceivin'."

I had expected her to say more, but instead she snatched a towel and wiped the sweat from her palms. Then she adjusted the plastic cape on the girl's shoulders and motioned her toward the other hair dryer. The magazine woman took her place in the chair and pointed to a picture on the wall.

"That's what I want," she said.

I saw Bert's expression. "Let's get your hair washed." She smiled. "Then after the conditioner is in for a few minutes, we can look and see what's what . . ."

Which meant that an alternative was already in the works. She positioned the woman's head over the basin and turned on the faucet. I heard her voice above the spray.

"So you say Laws was that busy. And even with Thea. I never woulda guessed it. Not in a million years. Used to drop by there once in while myself, you know."

I did not look at Bert but knew that a whole detailed history that Bert would share with me later would be extracted from the woman before the shampoo was rinsed out. I drained my cup and headed for the door.

Traffic had picked up and Eighth Avenue was clogged. The exhaust mingled with the heat radiating from the pavement, and standing under the shop's wide awning did not help. Five minutes later, I was still standing there when the door opened again and Bert stepped out to stand beside me.

"I got a conditioner on her now. Good for a few more minutes of gossip."

I nodded and said nothing. Finally, she said, "This heat gonna kill somebody." She watched the cars and continued. "Lotta old people who don't have no air-conditionin'."

I still waited.

Then: "Who you think did Laws in?"

"I have no idea," I said, looking at her.

"What do you think of that story about Thea?" Before I could answer, she went on. "Damn! What was goin' on in that girl's brain? She had Kendrick's nose open wide enough to grow a watermelon in; Michaels was actin' like she was the last bit of booty on the planet; and she was stickin' it to Laws, too? I mean, it's almost like she'd fuck a cactus if the wind blew one her way."

I still said nothing. As wild as that scene was, I couldn't imagine Thea being involved with Laws—not after Kendrick, who was so damn handsome you broke into a sweat just looking at him. I simply didn't believe it.

"Think they'll find who put Laws out?" Bert asked, still gazing down the avenue. The sun was in her eyes and she was sweating heavily.

chapter twelve

Dad was practicing downstairs when I came in. I went up to my room, stepped out of my sweaty clothes, and filled the tub with rose-scented bubble bath. What I really needed was to run naked at midnight into a crashing surf and then float on my back gazing up at the stars above the St. Croix landscape.

But that had been last summer, with Tad waiting on the beach, laughing as I waded back to him, telling me how crazy I was and how much he loved my craziness.

I needed to feel wet sand under my feet again, rubbing the stony calluses away from my sole. Or soul. Or both.

Right now, the man was as inaccessible as St. Croix. And there was no surf here in the city, so the warm bath and a Tina Turner CD would have to do.

I slid into the tub and rested my head back, feeling

the bubbles dissolve against my skin. I closed my eyes and naturally the phone rang, and naturally I reached for it quickly, hoping it would be Tad calling to say that he was on his way home, or better yet that he was already home and waiting for me. Dreams are like that.

It was Teddi Lovette finally getting around to doing what she'd promised to do several days ago.

"Mali. Sorry I couldn't get to you before now. We've been rehearsing pretty hard and—"

"Listen," I said, cutting into her apology. "I'd like to know what's going on. Why that thing about my joining the group? Why am I all of a sudden living in Brooklyn? What's going on?"

"Look, Mali. I'm sorry I had to do that to you. My mother—well, I'm having a problem with her. Or I should say, she has a problem."

"Let me guess. Anything to do with black folks?"

There was a pause in which I heard the intake of breath and then a light sigh. "I can't answer that."

"Why not?"

"I can't answer because I don't *have* an answer. Not yet, anyway."

"Does your mother know about Kendrick?"

"She met him, yes."

"Does she know . . . how you feel about him?"

"Well, I . . ."

"Come on, Teddi. It's all over your face. If I can see it, surely Mom can see it. The lady's no fool."

There was another silence and I knew I had hit a nerve.

"Well, I . . . Listen: this isn't why I called you. I

don't want to discuss my feelings for Kendrick. Not now, at least. I need to know something about Thea."

"But Thea's dead. She's gone. How can she—"

"I still need some information." There was another pause before she said, "I'll pay you to deliver it."

"Why is this so important to you?"

"I can't tell you that. The only thing I can say right now is that I need to know as much about her as I can."

"Like what?"

"Personal stuff. History. Things like that."

"What do you intend to do with it?"

"Nothing that'll hurt her, I can promise you that."

"How can you hurt a dead person?"

She didn't answer, but said, "I can also promise you twenty thousand if you get it for me."

"Dollars?"

"If that's not enough, let me know. I know it's going to be hard. Folks will say, 'Let the dead bury the dead,' but I need this."

"Damn."

"Will you do it, Mali? I hate to put a dollar amount on something like this, but it's the only way I know to help Kendrick."

"Why don't you get a private investigator?"

"I don't trust them. Sometimes they take your money and then go over to the other side."

"What other side?"

She did not answer again, but went on as if I'd never spoken. "I trust you, though."

"Me? Bullshit."

"Whatever you say, but you played along in front of my mother, and from that I knew I could trust you."

"Well, that act was as far as I'm willing to go."

"Listen, twenty thousand is a drop in the bucket for me, and—"

"Tell me something," I said, cutting her off again. "What would Mrs. Lovette say when she finds out her daughter is squandering all of those dollars on a dead black barmaid?"

"My mother—and her name is not Lovette—has nothing to do with my money, thank God. I have my own. A lot of it. And I'm not spending it on a dead black barmaid, but on a live black actor. Will you help me?"

I thought about what twenty thousand could do. Cover my tuition, a new wardrobe, maybe get to kick sand again on that beach in St. Croix.

"Listen," I said, "twenty thousand is a lot for what you're asking. I'll see what I can do if you send a check to Elizabeth Jackson, Kendrick's attorney, she's—"

Maybe it was the connection or the static or something, but I thought I heard her say, "I've already done that. I'm paying Kendrick's legal fees."

"Shit."

"Mali, I believe he's innocent. And you believe he's innocent just as I do. There's something in that girl's background that'll prove it."

"Like what?"

"Like if I knew, I wouldn't be asking you to find out. I'm counting on you."

The phone went dead and I slid back into the tub. All the bubbles had disappeared and I ran more hot water until I felt comfortable again. Then I reset the CD and Tina's voice filled the room. I hummed along to the sound of "Undercover Agent for the Blues."

chapter thirteen

I spent the next day, Saturday, enlarging the file I'd started the day after Kendrick had been arrested. I had amassed a fair amount of information: Thea's obit, the pageant, the funeral program, her pregnancy. On Kendrick's card, I noted his feelings (or lack thereof) regarding Teddi and cross-referenced her card with a check mark. Why would she want information on Thea? Would it help Kendrick or help her? I also looked at Flyin' Home's card again. I needed to find him. We needed to talk.

That evening, sitting in my room with all this stuff clogging my brain didn't help my mood. The house was empty and my footsteps echoed as I moved through the living room. Dad had a gig at the Club Harlem and I needed to be around people. Twenty minutes later, I stepped out of the shower and into the black dress he and I had fought over the day of the funeral.

Looking in the mirror, I had to admit that the

dress looked better in a midnight fog than at a high-noon function. Still, it would have to do until I got a real job or finished school. Or made up my mind to help Teddi. Twenty thousand dollars. I had visions of paying off my entire tuition bill. And seeing Dad smile when I finally received my doctorate.

"Benin and her husband are gone. It's you and me and Alvin now, and we gotta keep on keepin' on. . . ."

He had said this one morning when he'd come in and found me sitting on the sofa, gazing at Benin's picture on the mantel. She had nearly completed her master's studies in English literature. Her husband, William, had been a physician. But they'd gone on vacation and died in a hiking accident. Dad and I are raising their son. And holding on to memories.

Dad had made no secret of his disappointment when I had detoured from social work to join the NYPD. In fact, he had been mortified. And later he couldn't stop smiling when I'd gotten fired for hitting that cop.

"Now perhaps you'll do what you were meant to do."

So here I was, thirty-two and still facing the books. Still chasing another degree.

The black silk high-heel pumps that killed me on the rare occasions I was foolish enough to put them on seemed to have shrunk even more. But I loved them the way a woman might love the wrong man: ignore the bad construction and end up crippled or scarred for life. I got into them, practiced five minutes of biofeedback for foot pain, and willed myself to walk to the door. Outside, I'd hail a cab before I got to the curb. In the club, I planned to sit until dawn.

When the Club Harlem had opened the previous year, there had been great fanfare because for a while it was the only jazz supper club north of 110th Street. A few months later, placards began appearing in the windows of other restaurants up and down Seventh, Eighth, Lenox, and Fifth Avenues offering gospel breakfasts, jazz brunches, and West African high-life music with dinner.

Even the bar around the corner, with a crowd so tough it should have kept sawdust on the floor for the blood, advertised a "live" deejay on Thursdays, prompting speculation about his condition on the other nights.

The Club Harlem took note and quickly reduced their prices—and the size of their dinner plates—and with their fancy decor they managed to remain ahead of the game. Dad's ensemble was a regular and his name in the window guaranteed a full house on the weekends.

When I stepped out of the cab, I saw that the club's double-height brass inlaid doors were still graffiti-free, the evergreens on each side still swayed in the huge terra-cotta planters, and the maître d' still escorted patrons to the tables. The tourists had breathed more life into the area, and the weekend special prix-fixe jazz supper of broiled catfish, red rice, yams, and collard greens made the place busier than ever.

My table was off to the side but well within the sight line of the recessed stage in the center of the sloping floor. A minute after I had eased into my seat, I spotted TooHot striding up the aisle, heading for the door. He brushed by me in the dim light. I made out his angry expression and quickly tapped his arm.

"You all right?"

"Shit, no. I—" He peered closer and then shook his head. "Mali. Oh, I'm sorry. 'Scuse the language . . ."

"What's wrong?"

"Plenty," he murmured, looking around. "Mind if I join you?"

Without waiting for an answer, he pulled up the chair opposite me, sat down, took out a handkerchief, and dabbed at his dark forehead. His light gray silk suit gave off a discreet sheen against his dark shirt and white tie. He had checked his panama at the door.

"Mali, if I'd known I was gonna be bumped from my table 'cause a some damn tourist, I never woulda showed up tonight. No offense. You know I go for your pop's sounds, that's why I'm here. But this thing's gittin' outta hand. Everywhere you look, every corner, you trippin' over mobs a palefaces peepin' 'round, droolin' at the architecture, linin' up Sunday mornin' to sit in our churches, crowdin' us outta Sylvia's and Copeland's. We got more sightseein' buses up here than regular buses."

"But their money spends, you know, just like ours."

"Well I ain't sayin' otherwise, but don't come bustin' in like they got a court order or somethin'. It's like comin' into your house and pushin' you out your own bed."

I wanted to remind him that Harlem, Nieuw Haarlem as the Dutch had called it before the British snatched it from them and anglicized the name in 1664, was originally filled with Huguenots, Danes, Swedes, and Germans. The area was almost all-white until about 1910, six years after the IRT subway was completed.

Before that, most black folks were crowded in the Tenderloin District—24th Street to 42nd Street, west of Fifth Avenue. Or we were in Hell's Kitchen battling the Irish. But TooHot was too hot right now. He wanted his table, not a history session. He had a permanent spot here, front and center, that he'd paid for the same way wealthy folks paid for special pews in some churches. No matter how late they arrived, the space had better be there, available.

TooHot didn't have much of a grievance as far as I could tell. According to Dad, he was something of an outsider himself, having come to Harlem from St. Thomas in the fifties. And quicker than you could mouth the words "free enterprise," he had decided that pushing those garment-center Cadillacs nine-to-five straight-time wasn't his stick, and had promptly started taking the single action uptown for a Georgia boy named Pete "Walrus" Jackson.

TooHot had been known as Willie Jackson back then—no relation to Walrus—and had resembled a six-foot stick, so they called him Wee Willie. That stuck until the day he mistakenly popped into the Rock Tavern on Eighth Avenue near 117th Street where the cops were waiting in the back booth to discuss some overdue payments. The barmaid had looked around, then yelled the famous "Shit-it's-too-hot!" warning that sent Wee Willie in the wind.

Days later, he had resurfaced, rechristened, and had resumed business as usual, which after a time helped him buy a florist shop, a Laundromat, three brownstones, two cars, one condo, and one police sergeant. Now he sat here, acting ugly because other foreigners had stepped to his turf.

I raised my hand and a waiter appeared before I lowered it. "Walker black, straight up, and Absolut and orange, please."

The waiter disappeared and TooHot smiled. "You sound like a pro. Needed to put you behind the counter in the Half-Moon."

In the dim light, I didn't know if he was smiling or frowning, so I settled for the slight lift of his shoulders.

More people had come in and a line of standing-room-only patrons had gathered along the side walls waiting for the set to start. Their faces took on varying tints as the sconces above them flickered like candles.

The waiter returned and TooHot said, "Put this on my tab and bring another round. I'll be sittin' here tonight."

He drank slowly, lifting the glass several times to take small sips like a chef testing a new recipe. He made no sound at all.

I said, "Too bad about Laws . . . papers said it was robbery. What do you think?"

"I think that those who know ain't sayin' and those who sayin' don't know."

"Come on, TooHot, what does that mean?" I gave him my brightest smile but in the semidarkness its effect was lost.

"Just what I said," he replied.

"Okay." I sighed. "It's just that the place had such a bad-luck rep. Kendrick's in jail. Thea's dead. Now Laws. You'd think somebody was burning black candles in the basement and sticking pins through the walls."

He glanced at me quickly and I thought I saw a shade pass over his eyes. Superstition, strong enough, will motivate everyone.

"Well," he paused and looked around at the table nearest us. They were tourists, complete with accent, camcorder, and the ubiquitous street map folded into a manageable square near the glass of white wine. Satisfied they were not from the neighborhood, he leaned forward, his voice falling so that it was barely audible above the background hum.

"You ask me, Henderson Laws was lookin' for trouble."

"You mean with that private parade?"

He had raised his glass, then stopped. "You know about that?"

"Who doesn't?"

"Yeah, you right. Don't ask, don't tell. Till it's too late. Henderson was drivin' two ways on a one-way street. Took on all comers. I know 'cause I was in there every day."

"Every day?"

"Every day. He was one a my best customers. Don't know too many who'd lay half a yard a day each on two numbers: 252 and 148 were his favorites."

"Fifty dollars each? A hundred dollars a day?" I sat there, amazed, imagining what I could do with a hundred dollars a day.

The waiter returned with the second round. I had not finished my first, but TooHot, though he drank slowly, was ahead of me and going through the chef's testing ritual again.

"A yard a day ain't much," he said, "dependin' on what you takin' in. Laws didn't feel no weight 'cause he was pullin' a heavy dime."

"He ever hit?"

"Oh, yeah. Not too often 'cause he played 'em straight. Didn't combinate 'em like he did his other stuff." He smiled briefly and became serious again. "Laws used to say, 'When I hit, I want it heavy,' and that's what he got. Maybe three, four times in a year. Got so I had to spread his investment around with several bankers. Once or twice I rode his luck myself. You know how that goes."

I shrugged, never having played a number in my life. My math was so bad I could barely add up a grocery receipt. If I played a number and hit, I'd have a serious problem figuring how I did it. What would I get for betting a three-way number, or a six-way number? It was bad enough back in the day when you could play "the bolito," a two-way number. Now you can bet a four-way.

If I played and hit, I wouldn't know if it paid six

hundred, five hundred, or ten-to-one, and every time TooHot strolled by I'd be looking beady-eyed, thinking he had held out on me. So the best bet was to keep my dollar in my pocket and remain friends.

"With all that money," I said, "maybe somebody was trying to rob him. Had he hit recently?"

"No."

I watched him rub his chin as if trying to decide if he should continue. Then he said, "There's a little more to the story, though I can't figure how it fits."

"What?"

"Well, you know Henderson Laws was a jealous man."

"He was jealous of Thea?"

"No. Of Kendrick."

"Well, if Kendrick liked Thea, I guess—"

"No, no," he interrupted, waving his glass in a small circle. "Laws had eyes for Kendrick. Woulda licked dog-doo from the bottom of his Nikes if Kendrick had asked him."

"You're kidding."

"But Kendrick was straight-up. He wasn't interested. He woulda quit, been outta there long ago, but some time back Laws had talked him into borrowin' some dollars from him. Kendrick was into some Off Broadway production group or somethin' and needed funds. Laws, instead of becomin' one of the backers, loaned Kendrick a couple a grand, thinkin' he could buy him, I guess.

"Anyway, the production folded and Kendrick still owed Laws the dollars. So he was workin' there for

zip and tips and doin' his other gigs to make ends meet.
But you know how actors are. That bar job meant
nuthin' to him. Plus he liked Thea."

"And Thea was involved with Laws."

He raised his shoulders slightly and confirmed by
his silence what I didn't want to believe.

"Laws plus some others," he said finally.

I raised my glass and swallowed until it was
empty.

"She was a busy woman."

"No restriction on the friction," he said.

"What else do you know about her?" I asked.

"Not much."

He held up his hand for the waiter again, and
then another round was placed on the table.

"Listen, TooHot, I need an address."

"Who we talkin' about?"

"Flyin' Home."

He put his glass down and peered at me in the
dim light. "You mean wheelchair Flyin' Home?"

"Is there any other?"

"Mali, listen to me: Back off. I don't have to tell
you the boy's bad news."

"I know. I saw him the night Thea died. He—"

"What is it you want from him?"

"Information."

"Like what? Come on. Don't beat 'round the
bush."

"Like who he might've seen leaving the alley the
night Thea was killed."

"How you know that?"

"He told me he was there—or near there. He might know something."

"Whyn't you leave that to the five-oh. They'll get the wire sooner or later."

"Or never. And Kendrick'll remain in jail for something he didn't do. Come on, TooHot, I need this."

He rubbed his hands over his face, and in the dark I could see he was having trouble making up his mind. "Okay. Look, Mali, I'll put it on the drum. He'll find you, okay?"

The show was about to start. The lights dimmed further and the general hum of the patrons subsided.

"Here come your pop," TooHot whispered. The lights went out completely except for the spotlight on center stage, and TooHot joined in the applause with the enthusiasm of a schoolboy, completely forgetting my presence.

chapter fourteen

On the way home, if Dad had asked me what I'd thought of the set I would have had to lie. After listening to TooHot I couldn't concentrate on anything, and I had sat there allowing all the sounds, all the applause of the evening, to slip right past me.

Now I tried to get everything straight. Laws had been eyeing Kendrick while practicing with Thea. Probably out of spite, he accused Kendrick of killing her. But who really did her in? And after that, who had gotten to him? TooHot figured that with the private parade Laws had goin' on, it could've been anyone. It could've been the person that Flyin' Home might've seen near the alley.

That whole scene was like a swamp, dense and ugly, and I imagined unnameable creatures slithering through the murk. Had Thea known about Laws and his private parade? Did she know he'd had a thing for

Kendrick? Did she care? And Laws had to have known about Edwin Michaels, as hot as Michaels had been on Thea's tail. That floating eye didn't miss much.

I wondered how much of this news was worth repeating to Bert. Did she know that Kendrick's legal bill was being paid? Did she know about the money he had owed Laws? And she had been so calm when we'd talked about how Laws had been found leaking like a sieve from all those puncture wounds.

The cab let us out in front of the house and Ruffin greeted us as Dad unlocked the door, laid his bass against the sofa, and headed for the kitchen to brew his customary cup of coffee.

I crawled up the stairs to my bedroom and didn't have to look at the clock to know it was nearly 5 A.M. The sun was coming up and the chorus of birds, right on time, was already in motion and seemed to favor the branch nearest my window. Before I fell asleep, I made a note to climb that tree and cut down that branch.

My intentions must have been telegraphed on the wind because when I woke at 10 it was so quiet it scared me. I lay under the sheet wondering where the birds had gone. I was about to slip on my robe and check on Dad when the phone rang.

Let it be Tad, I thought. Let him say he's on his way home. Today.

It was Bertha, calling for an update on Laws.

"Nothing's new," I said, trying to hide my disappointment. "Tad's still away so I can't get any information. When the phone rang, I thought it was him."

"Well, let me get off the line. I don't want you missin' out. Talk to you later."

"No, wait a minute," I said before she disconnected. "What's goin' on?"

"Miss Viv dropped by the shop last night. You remember her?"

Indeed I did. She was the beautician who'd temporarily rented space from Bert the previous summer. Viv had been dumped by her boyfriend, the biggest dope dealer uptown, and in the process had lost her beauty shop to his new girl.

To even things up, Viv had spoken to me and dropped a dime to the Narcotics Strike Force. Things turned out all right for her, but not before I'd been caught in the middle.

"How could I forget her?" I asked. "What did she want?"

"Stopped by to say that Anne Michaels, the senator's wife, has an appointment at her place tomorrow. Special makeover or somethin'."

"I thought most shops are closed on Mondays."

I heard Bert sigh and suck air through her teeth. Then she said, "See, Mali, since you went and got your head scalped, you don't know what else is goin' on around here."

It was my turn to sigh. Since I had gotten all but two inches of my hair cut off a few years ago at the Klip Joint on 116th Street, Bert had nursed a feeling of betrayal, as if she'd lost a prized patron. My occasional drop-ins for scalp treatments couldn't make up for the loss, and she let me know it every so often. I tried to ignore the hurt tone.

"Maybe Anne Michaels wants a private day all to herself," I said.

"Naw. That ain't likely. Almost all the shops used to be closed on Mondays. Now almost all of 'em are open. Ain't nobody lettin' a dollar fly too far these days. Spends just as fast on Monday as it do on Tuesday. Your shop closed, you lose."

"Why do you think Anne's going there?"

"Well, that ain't hard to figure. It's election time. Edwin Michaels is rollin' into every bar and barbershop and block association in the phone book. I guess his wife is trippin' on the beauty-shop circuit. Get her hair together at Viv's place, nails done at Darlene's, toes at Dee's Pedi-care, and eyebrows at Beryl's Braids 'n' Locks Beauty Shop."

"What about your place?"

"Hell no. She ain't no Queen Anne on no royal-ass tour, even though she tryin' hard to act like one. My place way too small for her, and besides, she already know by now that Thea used to come here and Kendrick's my brother. She ain't lookin' to handle no scandal."

"So she's headed for Viv's tomorrow?"

"About twelve noon."

I hung up the phone. Senator Michaels was usually a shoo-in, but this time around he was up against a young tough-talking challenger named Dora Peterson, an activist attorney who was questioning the senator's record page-by-page and picking it apart line-by-line. She now had Edwin Michaels doing the unthinkable— getting into the streets and actually meeting his constituents.

Either the hill at 145th Street and Bradhurst Avenue had gotten a little steeper or I had gotten a little older. The heat pressed in as I hiked past Jackie Robinson Park, listening to the screams and laughter of the children in the pool, punctuated by splashing and the whistle of the lifeguards. The sound resonated above the bedlam of traffic, and the pool water sparkled in the ninety-degree heat.

I felt my sweat gather in a pool of its own before trickling down the small of my back. I consoled myself with the thought that the Pink Fingernail would be fully air-conditioned in honor of Anne Michaels's visit.

The shop was on Amsterdam Avenue about a dozen doors from 145th Street, and adjoining a new barbershop. There was a soul-food take-out restaurant, a small bodega, and a check-cashing business nearby. A block away, in a lush triangle of green dedicated to the jazz singer Johnny Hartman, a few men sat with chessboards balanced between them. Others lounged on the periphery trying to beat the heat and life in general with small brown-bagged bottles.

In one year Viv's shop had undergone a change. The only thing I recognized was the door, except now the frame around the glass was edged in a deeper pink quilted plastic. There was also a large brass knocker, but that was only for show; it didn't move and you still had to ring the bell and be buzzed in.

When I pressed the bell, it felt sticky. The door opened and I stepped into the cooled atmosphere as if someone had been chasing me. Viv was surprised then glad to see me.

"How come you haven't dropped in before now?" she asked, shaking her head. The mirrored panels reflected the blond strands woven into her braids. Her face was still pretty but she seemed to have gained more weight and probably tipped the scale now at two hundred even. She took my arm and led me farther inside.

"Sisters," she announced to the six beauticians, "this is Mali, my good friend."

The women smiled, then turned back to their customers. Word had gotten around that the politician's wife was scheduled, and the place was crowded, though Anne Michaels had not arrived yet. A long table against the wall opposite the workstations held a large coffee urn, a stack of real china cups and saucers, platters of croissants, cold cuts, cheese dips, and two half watermelons filled with fruit.

The huge chandelier that had dominated the old shop had been removed and the walls were now paler than the blinding pink of last summer. I listened to Barry White's sensual promises float out slow and deep from speakers no larger than the palm of my hand.

"You made some changes," I said.

"You noticed?" She seemed pleased as she led me through the shop. "When I got the place back, I fired all those no-behind skinny girls that bitch had in here. Sittin' up profilin' while the place goin' down the damn drain. But who cared. Well, now my ex is RIP, his bitch is history, and I'm back."

She waved her hands to take in the scene. "I got big plans, Mali. This is a substantial business and I brought in some substantial sisters. As they say, we large and in charge."

Miss Viv was true to her word. The new operators were plus-size beauty queens and not one weighed in under one seventy-five, and they perched on solid wrought-iron stools. When one left her station to get a towel, the fringe on the ankle-length wrap skirt flowed east-west as her feet moved north-south.

"And look at this," Viv said, opening a side door and stepping into the adjoining barbershop. "Place was nuthin' but a messed-up pile of bricks so I took it, and look at it now."

This space was smaller, with four female barbers at work. Floor-to-ceiling mirrors reflected a brick wall, white counters, black leather upholstery, and a black terrazzo tile floor. Instead of Barry White, a forty-six-inch screen showed green-haired Dennis Rodman pounding down the court from a rebound.

We stepped back into the beauty salon and she turned to me again. "You welcome to stop in anytime, Mali. Haircut, manicure, pedicure, facial. It's on me. I'll never forget what you did for me."

"Listen," I said, "that barmaid who was killed in the Half-Moon?"

"Thea?"

"Yes. Do you know anything about her?"

"Naw. Nuthin' serious. 'Cause you know I'm tryin' to keep my own head on straight and get this place back together. I didn't have no time to be poppin' in the Half-Moon or anywhere else. But there was a lotta talk goin' 'round here the day she died."

"Like what?"

"Well, like how she was kinda strange. You know how some sisters can run hot and then cold? Talk was that she ran hot and cold at the same time. Could lay a man in the morning and don't want to even know his name come evening."

"Just like some brothers . . ."

"Yeah, except in her case, her juice musta been kickin' 'cause she sure had 'em comin' back, sometimes down on all fours."

"Anybody in particular?"

"Well, word is that one of 'em was the husband of a certain lady who's due to walk in here any minute."

The bell rang on cue. Someone pressed the buzzer and Anne Michaels swept through the door with another woman in her wake.

"Listen," Viv whispered, "talk was that Thea had somethin' in the oven."

She left me standing slack-jawed as she moved forward, smiling, to greet the senator's wife. How had she known Thea was pregnant? I marveled at the power of the drum, then felt nervous, wondering how the word had gotten out.

It was all I could do to focus on the visitors. Anne was medium height, slim and brown, expensively dressed in a mid-calf-length yellow linen skirt and sleeveless top, and moved with an attitude that was too cool to pass for elegance. She was in her early forties with flawless skin and a posture that spoke of hours of tennis and swimming.

The other woman, whom Anne introduced to Viv as Rita Bayne, her husband's assistant, was short and stocky and seemed to bend under the weight of a large canvas shoulder bag. Her thick curled hair fell into her face and the rhinestone-edged eyeglasses dangling around her neck clicked against her beaded necklace as she headed for the refreshment table.

"So this is the Pink Fingernail." Anne smiled, glancing around as if she'd just come to town yesterday and had heard none of its history. "What a lovely place. And so busy. I'm so glad you were able to fit me in."

I glanced at Viv and wondered how she was going to get through this appointment. Like Miss Bert, she smiled sometimes but didn't take bullshit anytime.

"I'm glad you like the place," Viv said, then immediately launched into a speech that she'd been wanting, it seemed, to deliver all her life.

"Hard work'll get you where you wanna go, and I'm doin' all right but we need more business loans in this community. Harlem ain't dead, contrary to all those reports. What we need is money to open more places where our money will stay where we spend it, you know what I mean? This neighborhood is—"

"I understand," Anne Michaels said, adroitly cutting Viv off. "As a matter of fact . . ." She glanced around, and for a second I expected to hear the snap of her fingers. Instead, she parted her teeth in a wide smile and said, "Rita, where are those brochures?"

I wanted to laugh. When did a Harlemite ever need a brochure to tell them what was wrong with Harlem and what needed fixing? Senator Michaels had been in office for twelve years, long enough for him to have addressed at least *some* of the issues.

Rita separated herself from her plate long enough to rummage through the canvas bag and produce a stack of flyers and pamphlets, which she proceeded to distribute. She placed the remainder on the table and quickly returned to her plate.

Anne Michaels glanced at Rita, and the corner of her mouth lifted slightly before she looked away. Viv caught the look and I watched her take a deep breath in an effort to maintain her cool. Finally she said, "Mrs. Michaels, would you care for some coffee?" She did not wait for a reply, but called out, "Come, ladies, help yourselves. Please."

And turning to Anne Michaels again, she continued, "Now let's see. How about a facial to begin with, and then—"

"Well, I was thinking of a manicure." Anne Michaels smiled, looking at her watch. "Just a manicure for me. But Rita . . ." The sweep of her hand took in the whole of the assistant's shapeless figure. The gesture was casual and cruel and every woman in the shop, except Rita, saw and recognized it.

Viv stared at Anne again and I imagined her vote at that moment veering toward Dora Peterson. Rita walked over and positioned herself in a chair.

"Now," Viv asked softly, "what would you like done, Honey?"

Rita stared in the mirror, then looked away. "I don't really know. I never had time for anything like this. I can't remember when I—I mean I usually do my hair myself, you know? And my nails. I never do them."

Her voice was small and apologetic and seemed not to belong to her. She leaned back in the chair and I watched a faint nervous tic play at the corner of her mouth as Viv started to comb through the thick hair.

"Girl, you got beautiful hair. Women would kill for this stuff, you know? We gonna get it shaped up, conditioned, maybe put a little highlight in it . . ."

Doug DesVerney, a popular Harlem photographer, walked in and the makeover session morphed into a celebration—as if Michaels had already won the election. The other women, animated by the flash of the camera, filled their plates, smiling as Barry White let them know that it was all right to go for that third piece of pastry.

The photographer captured the scene as Viv hummed and worked wonders with Rita's hair, rolling the wet strands back from her face and trimming the unruly edges, apparently satisfied that her shop had been included in Anne's itinerary. Viv's smile was caught in the camera's flash, and now I couldn't tell which way she had decided to vote.

I glanced at Anne, who was examining her nails

under the manicurist's lamp. She looked around, and
when her gaze came to rest on her husband's assistant,
the faint trace of energy faded to a flat stare. But Viv
was applying a facial now. Rita's eyes were closed and
her rhinestone glasses were lying folded in her lap.

chapter fifteen

I left the Pink Fingernail and called Gladys Winston. She came on sounding not at all like Gladys Winston, and I strained to hear her against the noise of the traffic.

"Gladys? This is Mali. I haven't spoken with you since the funeral. Everything was handled very well."

"Thank you, but I felt I was barely there. My doctor had given me medication so I managed to get through that day. I planned to send acknowledgments, especially to your father. He spoke so eloquently. But right now, I don't know. I'm usually very organized, but at the moment I feel overwhelmed . . ."

"I wouldn't worry about that. You did more than what was expected."

"Well, the task now is to sort through her stuff and . . ."

"Are you the executor?"

"Yes, and just cutting through the red tape tired me out."

I nodded, knowing that before she'd been allowed to break the seal on Thea's apartment, she'd had to obtain a property voucher from the precinct, take it to the state tax bureau, then go to Surrogate's Court with the death certificate and other documents in order to obtain more documents, and finally submit everything to the property clerk's office.

"You have no idea how exhausting the process is," Gladys said. "A day or so ago, I took boxes to Thea's apartment, but that was as far—"

"I'll be glad to help you," I said, recognizing a once-in-a-lifetime chance. "I know how it was sorting through my sister's effects. It isn't something you'd want to do alone. You need to have someone who wasn't close to Thea, someone who could be objective . . . to help you. Sometimes it's just too many memories."

"I appreciate your offer. I've put it off long enough. I—"

"When do you want to do this?"

"Well, I was thinking about tomorrow, perhaps."

"I'll be there," I said quickly, allowing no space for a change of mind. "What time?"

"Okay. Around noon."

She gave me the address and hung up.

I let a minute pass before I picked up the phone again and dialed Elizabeth Jackson. She came on cool, crisp, and professional until she heard my voice, then said, "Hey, girl, I was trying to reach you. I already told Bertha . . ."

"What?"

"Autopsy confirmed Thea was three months pregnant."

"Then it's true." I sighed. "I even heard the news from Miss Viv at the Pink Fingernail."

"Did she happen to know who the father might've been?"

"She didn't say but I'm going to Thea's apartment tomorrow. With Gladys Winston. Maybe something'll turn up."

"Good. Lots of stuff to be found in nooks and crannies, not to mention what might be under the carpet and the mattress."

"I know where to look. I just need the opportunity. How's Kendrick?"

"The same. He mentioned your visit and how you might have someone, a witness."

"I'm not sure about this guy being a witness. Maybe he didn't see anything. Maybe he did and at the time was into some shaky stuff and won't want to talk at all. Tad's due back soon. Maybe he can pull the guy in for questioning. Meanwhile, I'm trying to locate him myself. Maybe he'll talk to me."

"I hope so. Kendrick's about at the end of his rope."

"I hear someone special is handling his expenses."

"Damn. The drums are working overtime. Anyway, it's an actress who must have a part interest in a gold mine. Walked in the office and dropped dollars that still have me blinking."

"Indeed."

"Indeed. I had to check her to make sure it wasn't crack cash. Seems she'd married a Wall Street man who was old as water, and on their honeymoon three years ago his emotion couldn't take the motion. Ticker quit and he went out with a smile. Now Miss Thing is kicking back, making merry with millions."

"And wants to make it with Kendrick."

"Too bad. I was kind of eyeing the brother myself. Making plans to make a move when all this is over and he walks. He's so fine I would've done the work pro bono. But hey, the girl has dollars that hollers. . . ."

"Well, her dollar might holler but the echo's not that deep. Kendrick's not interested in her. And Thea had nothing—in the bank, that is—but he loved her and would've eaten that bullet for her. So money, as they say, ain't everything."

Graham Court at 116th Street and Seventh Avenue was an eight-story monolith of marbled halls and four columned entrances facing an interior court. It was built at the turn of the century by William Waldorf Astor for upper-class New Yorkers and was the last major apartment building in Harlem to become integrated.

In 1928 the wrought-iron gates swung open to its first black tenant, but the Gothic gray-stone structure did not collapse as some had predicted. Since then, Graham Court had had several notable black tenants, among them Zora Neale Hurston.

When I approached the building, Gladys climbed out of her car. The only hint that she was prepared for heavy-duty house-cleaning was the Hermés scarf covering her hair. Other than that, she seemed more prepared for a trip downtown for a heavy-duty clean-out of Saks.

Up close, the skin around her eyes looked puffy, and her voice was still subdued.

"Glad you could make it. I'm really glad."

I followed her into the interior court and walked around the large planted area in the center of the circular drive. We entered the building on the far side and took the elevator to the eighth floor. Thea's apartment was large and light-filled with two bedrooms facing Seventh Avenue and a kitchen, dining room, living room, and small den looking out on the shops and restaurants of Little Africa on 116th Street.

Gladys disappeared into one of the bedrooms, leaving me to stand in the middle of the living room wondering why I had come. My presence now seemed like an intrusion.

There's something about a person that remains long after the person is gone. I remembered opening a drawer in Benin's bedroom and being stunned by the inescapable scent of Shalimar, the only perfume she'd ever worn. Faint as it had been, it resonated through the room, cutting me with a feeling of loss, love, and abandonment. My sister was gone, yet her essence was still there, contained in that drawer. And I had sat on her bed staring at the wall for an hour before I realized she wasn't going to walk into the room.

When Gladys reappeared I was surprised to see her in a pair of old jeans, flat shoes, and a T-shirt.

"I have some clothes here," she said, looking at me. "There were times when Thea couldn't stand to be alone. When she called me, I came over."

She walked into the other bedroom and I remained where I was.

Couldn't stand to be alone. With all the men in her life, when had Thea ever been alone . . . ?

I began to wonder how Gladys really fit into the puzzle of Thea's life. When Gladys had walked into Bertha's shop that day, she'd been ready to beat down anybody even remotely connected with Thea's death. Pretty strong emotions until Bertha had offered to straighten her out with that straightening comb.

"How often did Thea feel that way?" I asked when she stepped back into the room to open a small cabinet and pull out a fifth of Dewar's and two glasses.

"Quite often. Sometimes, I'd be here two, maybe three times a week. . . ."

I nodded. The bad thing about lying is that we have to work to remember the lie. In her office, she'd said something entirely different. Maybe it had been the vodka fogging her memory.

I watched her now as she poured the Scotch, handed me a glass, and sat down on the sofa. The living room was large and expensively furnished. The sofa, a camelback gray ultrasuede number, was soft enough to disappear in if you sat down too hard. Two brown

leather ottomans flanked the tiled fireplace and a large
square of glass rested on a low rough-cut granite base in
the center of the room. A small Catlett sculpture was on
the marble mantel next to a small Bose sound system,
and a series of Jacob Lawrence paintings covered the
wall over the sofa. There were no superfluous toys such
as cell phone, TV, or CD player, unless they were con-
cealed in one of the cabinets.

Not bad for a barmaid. Not bad at all, I thought as
I took a sip and put the glass down. Scotch was not my
favorite drink and I needed a clear head if I was to look
for anything.

"Where shall we start?" I asked.

"We'll each take a room. You start in there," she
said, pointing toward one of the bedrooms. "There are
boxes in the foyer."

I left her sitting on the sofa and entered the bedroom. It was the smaller of the two and I stood near the
door. Something was missing. A minute later, I realized
that there was no intimacy, no sense of life or living,
anywhere in the apartment. It was cold and sterile despite the sunlight splashing across the bed piled with
damask quilts and tasseled pillows. The place was a
decorator's showcase roped off from human emotion.

There was no bedroom clutter, personal pictures,
or small trays on the dresser where broken earrings or
unpaid bills accumulated, yet Thea had lived here for
several years.

Her death had been a public spectacle and everyone knew how she died, but few knew how she had
lived. Had she lived at all? Or simply floated through

the present like a ghost, not touching, feeling, seeing, or
wanting anything, a figment of the imagination of all
the people she'd come in contact with? But I knew she
had wanted something, because her hostility was unmis-
takable the night, several years ago, when she'd met me
at the club.

"So this is your dad?"

So what? Why get attitude? Had she wanted him
as a lover? Had she wanted him at all? Or was she
simply jealous because he was my father and perhaps
she hadn't known her own.

I could not feel her presence here so it was easy to
start opening every drawer in the dresser and chest. I
quickly poked through lingerie, sleepwear, sweaters,
blouses, and scarves, listening the entire time for Gladys.
Then I refolded each piece and placed them in the boxes
I'd dragged from the foyer.

I tiptoed to the door and heard Gladys in the next
room. She had turned on a small radio, and the music
muffled her movements. I went to the dresser again and
quickly slipped my hand behind the mirror but came up
with nothing, not even a dust ball. Whoever did the
cleaning, I'd certainly like to bring them over to my
place.

I pulled each empty drawer out again and turned
them over, looking for envelopes or papers that might
be taped to the undersides. Nothing. In the closet, two
dozen shoe boxes were stacked three rows deep on the
floor. I flipped the covers and saw beautiful shoes, size
7, which made me mad thinking of my own size 10s.

I went back to the chest and eased it away from

the wall. Because of the carpet, the chest barely moved. I leaned against it and squeezed my arm behind the small space. Nothing. I still heard the music from the adjoining bedroom but no movement. Maybe Gladys had given up and was simply sitting there, lost in memory. I needed to work faster because there was no telling when she might decide she'd had enough for one day.

My work on the force had taught me that most folks hid stuff in their bedrooms and most of the time at eye level. I sat on the edge of the bed and looked around, then leaned back and poked the long tapestry-covered bolster. It was solid stuff, whatever it was made of. I passed my fingers over the quilted headboard, and along the edge felt a small zipper. I opened it, eased my hand into the sliver of space, and extracted a small plastic freezer bag containing a bankbook.

Something was wedged between the pages but I didn't have time to look. I tiptoed to the door again, listening, then lifted my shirt and the pouch disappeared in the pocket of my jeans. I adjusted my shirt and called out.

"What would you like me to do next?"

There was no answer and I moved toward the other bedroom. Gladys sat on the bed with a small notebook on her lap and a half dozen letters spread out beside her.

"What would you like me to do?" I repeated.

This time she looked up. "Sorry, I . . . didn't hear you." She snapped the notebook closed and stuffed it along with the letters into a large shoulder bag. "I'll take care of this room. Did you get to the other closet, the one in the den? The boxes are already in there."

I watched her bury the shoulder bag on the chair beneath the dress she had worn and knew there was no way I could get to it, not even if she went to the bathroom. I'd have to make do with whatever information the bankbook held.

From the look on Gladys's face, I wondered if the notebook might have been Thea's diary or journal. Whatever she'd just read wasn't sitting too well with her.

"Everything okay?" I asked.

"Yes. Yes, fine."

"Where's the bathroom?"

"There's one in here and there's one off the foyer."

I chose the one off the foyer and left her sitting there. I locked the door and looked around, noting with small satisfaction that Thea and I had at least one thing in common: large old tiled bathrooms with deep, claw-footed tubs, old tulip-shaped basins, and toilets that sounded like the ocean when you flushed.

I sat on a small velvet-covered bench and quickly unwrapped the plastic. The bankbook had a balance of over a hundred thousand dollars with three entries a month of a thousand dollars on the first, tenth, and twentieth for the last three years. There was also a small faded photograph of an old woman.

I heard Gladys moving down the foyer, and I quickly flushed the toilet and washed my hands with a gel that filled the room with the scent of lilacs. I stepped out to see Gladys in the living room refilling her glass. I picked up my own and drank it down.

"Let's call it a day," she said. "Maybe come back next week."

"That's good," I said. "We can't do everything all at once."

chapter sixteen

ladys dropped me off at home. In my bedroom, I put the plastic pouch in my desk next to the other file, wondering if Thea had accumulated this nest egg from Michaels, Laws, or her husband, Roger.

When the phone rang I answered it quickly, grateful for the distraction.

"Mali? Hello baby . . ."

"Tad? Where are you?"

"Newark. Just arrived. But I've got good news and some bad news."

"Wait," I whispered, holding out my hand as if he had just stepped in the room. "Don't tell me now. You're back and that's it. I can wait for the bad news."

"Did you miss me?"

Did I miss him. I held the phone so close my ear ached. Did I miss him. His voice, the sound of him, flowed toward me like a train in a tunnel and everything seemed in danger of collapsing from the vibration.

I sat down. My back was wet and a tight urgent feeling was already blooming near the bottom of my stomach. Did I miss him.

"You're at Newark?" I asked again, just to hear the sound of him.

"Yeah. I'm hopping a cab. See you in a little bit."

I couldn't figure out how long a cab took to get from Newark to Harlem, but when I hung up it took two minutes to fill my bath and slide into a bank of hibiscus-scented foam.

One hour later the bell rang and I shooed Ruffin into the dining room and opened the door. Tad was standing there and I felt the ache even in my bones. His arms closed on me and I breathed in the familiar mint scent. His mouth was near my ear.

"Mali. Mali. Baby. Damn you look good I missed you my bag's in the cab come on over to my place damn you look good your dad home get your keys come on Baby . . ."

One urgent, strung-together rush of expression. No time to reply, no time to say, No Dad's not home he went to see the movie *Sankofa* with Miss Laura and yes we'll go to your place where I'll step out of my panties—why did I put them on in the first place I knew you were coming—step out of them and step into you and drown myself in the scent and smell and odor and musk and whatever else it is about you that makes me laugh and cry and sweat and act so damn crazy.

The cabbie was a polite Pakistani who pretended to concentrate on the traffic as my wrap skirt came off in the backseat. He coughed discreetly when we pulled

up in front of Tad's place and nearly shook Tad's hand
in response to the generous tip. Upstairs, Tad moved
through the apartment opening the windows and the
door to the terrace.

"Rather have the AC on?"

I'd rather have *you* on, I wanted to say, but I
smiled instead. "Whatever you like . . . is all right
with me."

The breeze from the river blew in like a blast of
steam, but I didn't mind it. Tad brought two drinks,
vodka and cranberry in tall ice-filled glasses, and sat
near me on the sofa.

"What's the news?" I asked, not really wanting an
answer. The California sun had burned the skin of his
face, neck, and arms to dark copper, but I was interested in the color below his belt buckle. He handed me
a glass.

"Okay. The good news is, I'm back. The bad news
is it's only for one day. We had a break in training and I
jumped the first thing smokin'."

I put my glass down and stared at him. "One day?
You're only here for one—?" My throat had drawn so
tight it hurt. He saw my expression and his arms came
around me and he buried his head in my neck, whispering, "Baby, listen: I know, it's only one day. But I had to
see you . . . Damn, girl. I was starving. I didn't care
how long it took. I had to come home. I didn't realize
how much I—"

I held him and it was a minute before I found my
voice. When I did, I was ready to scream. Instead I

surprised myself and murmured. "How much longer is this training going to take?"

He's only here for one day. Inside me, a dull ache flared. I had visions of him returning to L.A. and remaining there for the rest of the summer, possibly fall. Maybe winter. I pictured snowy sidewalks here in the city and only a phone call to connect me to the warmth of his voice.

He's here for one day.

I tried to breathe in and out, allowing the anger to slowly dissipate. Then I leaned away and gazed at him. I loved this man and right now we scarcely have time to love, talk of love, make love.

I watched him reach for his glass, and for a tight second my thoughts wandered. I could not even think now of approaching him about Kendrick and Flyin' Home. I'd need more time to work through his anger and persuade him to reach beyond his jealousy to help a man in danger of spending the next several years in prison.

When he spoke, his voice seemed as if he was already moving away from me, back to L.A.

"Mali, I know you're upset, but it'll soon be over. Since the bombings in Oklahoma and Atlanta, it seems every agency's on code red and rushing to retrain its personnel. I know how you feel; I feel just as bad. I'll make it up to you when I'm home for good."

He put his glass down again without taking a drink and drew me toward him. His eyes were half-closed and he began to massage the small place in my lower back. His hands were strong and powerful and the rhythm in my chest began to skip and I felt if we did not see his bed in the next five minutes, I'd be ready to perform my own act of terrorism. I didn't take a drink either. I wanted to be wide awake when I did it.

"I almost forgot. I bought you something," he whispered, dropping his hands and moving from the sofa. He extended a package and I opened it, pulled out the items, and held them up in the light: black garter belts, old-fashioned and beautiful and made of intricately woven, cobweb-like lace.

"I understand they still wear these in Paris," he whispered. "The saleslady said they're very healthy."

"Healthy?" I looked at him, searching for the pun.

"Yeah, you know: She said ordinary pantyhose interfere with your circulation . . . or something . . ."

I gazed at him and saw behind his smile, the need to see me laugh, and when I did the tightness in my throat eased and I reached into the bag again and pulled out lace-topped stockings with black seams and heels outlined in tiny rhinestones. I didn't know Tad would dare step inside Victoria's Secret.

"Where am I supposed to wear these?" I asked.

He was standing now and easily pulled me up from the sofa. "From here to there," he whispered, drawing a line toward the bedroom.

I didn't think it was possible to construct an entire world within the four walls of a single room and shut out everything else. I dialed Dad and left a short message on the machine: "Tad's back for one day. I'm at his place."

Then I dropped the receiver by the side of the bed and for the rest of the time nothing else existed.

The heat of the afternoon melted into evening cool and at night the horn of a lone tugboat wafted in on the silence and then it was gray again and then morning light before we noticed.

I rolled over and lay my head on Tad's chest. He was quiet now, asleep. Earlier, his heart had drummed loud and fast against me, as if he'd been running.

In the half-light I watched the slight rise and fall of his stomach. My finger traced the fine line of hair below his navel and I wondered why I felt so oddly dissatisfied.

He stirred, and his voice came to me in a whisper. "Mali, I'm sorry about this. This is like snatching something on the run. Maybe I should've waited until I was back for good and we had more time. Maybe—"

"No. No." I eased up on one elbow to look at him. "If you only came back for five minutes, it's more than what I had before you got here. You're leaving tonight. There wasn't time to talk about anything. I love you . . . I love you . . ."

"Ah, Baby." He slipped his arms around me and lay down again, but I knew it was me, my fault and not his. I could not concentrate, knowing that he would be furious when he found out I had been trying to help Kendrick.

• • •

I refused to go with him to the airport because that would have meant returning home alone and I couldn't do that. So I showered and smiled and dressed and somewhere in the small talk heard myself whisper good-bye, and closed the door and concentrated on the irregular pattern in the terrazzo floor as I walked to the elevator.

It was dark out. And cool. As if a new season had sneaked in behind my back. On 135th Street, I walked past the brightly lit windows of Lenox Terrace. There was a crowd inside Twenty-Two West, the neighborhood bar. I peeked in and a wave of regret washed over me; we'd had no time for dinner. The vodka and cranberry on the table had warmed as the ice melted and overflowed and made circles on the table that I'd tried to clean up. We'd had no time.

"You'll come out to L.A. for a few days. Your dad won't mind a few days."

And I remembered saying yes, if you're not home in a week, we'll work it that way. I continued to walk and crossed to the other side of 135th Street, away from the bar. Behind me the tall outline of the Rivington Apartments and Delano Village stood out against the velvet sky as I headed west toward Malcolm X Boulevard. The lights were out in the Bennet playground and the moonlight cut through the line of trees to cast gray slivers along the empty benches. I passed the handball area and someone called out.

"Heard you was lookin' for me."

Just inside the high chain-link fence, Flyin' Home was waiting near the entrance. The dogs lay beside his chair, half-hidden behind the row of benches. I stepped into the shadows, moving quickly toward his voice.

"TooHot said you wanted to see me," he said. "What's up?"

"Yes, I—"

"Make it quick, Mali. I got stuff to do. If it was anybody but you, I wouldn't be here . . ."

He glanced around at the slight rustling sounds of the wind in the branches overhead, then folded his arms, waiting.

"I need to know if you saw anything the night Thea died," I said quickly.

He looked at me and rubbed the side of his face, still glancing around. "Like I told you, you ain't on the force no more. Why you want to know?"

I leaned against the low railing opposite him. I was no longer on the force but he and I both knew I had treated him with respect all the times he had been hauled in with clothing and cameras and TVs and jewelry that hadn't belonged to him. And when that blast ended his career, I'd still tried to help him. He was a thief but he'd never put a gun to a nose, a knife to a chest, or a cord around anyone's neck.

"We both know I'm not on the force, but we also know that a brother's down at the Dee for something he didn't do. I need to know if you saw anything—a man, woman, a car."

"I seen both."

"A man and a woman?"

"No. A car and a person. The person who came out the alley. Moved slow so I didn't make nuthin' of it. The streetlight was out so I couldn't tell you if it was man or woman. They walked normal, wasn't tryin' to beat no clock, you understand. They got into a small black car. By its headlight I guessed it mighta been a foreign number. I don't know. Ain't had time to think about it then 'cause Sheba here sat down. I mean this big dog just stopped cold. Set up a howl so bad I knew right away some shady shit had just went down, you know what I'm sayin'. Then Solomon here, he join her. So with all that, plus the *siren song* comin' from the five-oh, I was outta there."

"But why'd you leave? Why didn't you tell the cops what you saw?"

"Me?" He pointed to his chest and looked at me as if I'd asked him to rise up and walk again. "Listen, Mali: You know I got a sheet long as your legs. They take me down and shake me up and all my shit fall out. I wasn't ready for that, not that night."

"Okay, that was then. This is now. Would you be willing to speak to someone I know? A detective?"

He glanced at me and shook his head emphatically. "Mali, you and me go back a long way. You helped me when nobody else would. But I ain't lookin' to git jammed on no jive tip."

"Okay," I said. I was quiet for a moment, then tried another approach. "Suppose that person saw you?"

"What person?"

"The one who left the alley."

"They did! They did see me! That's why I'm only

out at certain hours. I'm real careful, 'cause that was probably a hit. I don't know what went down but I know I don't wanna be next."

He clicked his teeth and the dogs rose. "So you can see where I'm at, Mali. Kendrick's my man, but I can't do nuthin', not a damn thing."

I stood at the entrance as he left the park. He'd had no time to pick up speed when a car that had been double-parked with its engine idling now eased along the street beside him. I spotted the glint of steel as the window slid down.

"Flyin'! Look out!" I screamed and ran up to the wheelchair. The gun went off and Flyin' went down. The gun went off again, this time aimed at me. But I had dropped to the ground before the slug pierced the NO PARKING sign above my head.

The car then made a screeching U-turn, heading now for the Harlem River Drive. I managed to get up as two boys walking through the ball court came running. Twenty-two West emptied out and patrons dodged traffic to get to us only to be held at bay by the snarling dogs. The chair was overturned and the dogs circled it with bared teeth.

"Somebody call 911!" I shouted as I crouched down to move toward the chair. The dogs bared their teeth wider and I moved no farther. "Flyin'?" I shouted. "Are you hit? Answer me."

He clicked his teeth softly and the dogs moved back, allowing me to crawl to him on my hands and knees. "Don't try to move. Keep still. The ambulance'll be here. It's right around the corner."

"Listen, Mali," he whispered. "Unfasten me from the chair and set it straight. Unfasten me, quick!"

I did as I was told, working fast, thinking perhaps that the strap was cutting into him, twisting his body in a painful position. He lay on the ground now and I uprighted the chair.

Flyin' suddenly lifted himself up on one elbow and called out, "Sheba! Go, girl!" And Solomon followed. The two dogs, barking and snarling and pulling the empty chair, plunged through the crowd, who fell over themselves in a panic trying to move out of the way. In a second, the dogs were gone.

Flyin' sank back and I cradled his head in my lap. "They know the way," he whispered. "Somebody home take care of 'em till I git on my feet. Ain't that funny? 'Till I git on my feet' . . . yeah, that's some funny shit."

I untied the scarf around his throat and he held it to his shoulder where the blood was now spreading like a red blossom. But he was still conscious.

"Flyin', who was after you? Who?"

He rolled his eyes and it was a second before they came back in focus. "Don't know. That's the same car was at the alley. Same car. You be cool, Mali, 'cause if they seen me that night, they probably followed and seen me talkin' to you. They seen you too. You know what I'm sayin'?"

The EMS technicians shouldered their way through the crowd, ignoring a man who called, "What took you so long? You right up the block? Coulda walked here, dammit!"

Someone else yelled back, "Aw, shut the fuck up and let 'em do they job."

The man turned around, looking into the crowd for the caller. "Yo! You don't chill, EMS be havin' *two* jobs. You be in that ammalambs with 'em! I'll help you!"

The technicians ignored everyone and got Flyin' onto the stretcher as the police arrived and took a statement from me. The ambulance siren started up, and instead of backing out into the now-crowded street, it moved quickly along the sidewalk and turned onto Lenox Avenue toward the hospital.

The crowd began to disperse, leaving behind bits of opinions and whispered observations. "Knew he was gonna git smoked sooner or later. He the one lifted my TV couple years ago."

"Damn! How he do that in a chair."

"Wasn't in no chair then. Went in the wrong crib and came out carryin' a bullet."

"Maybe tonight somebody tried to finish the job."

"That, or they tryin' to git to what's *under* that chair. Flyin' Home carry some UPS—ultrapure, underpriced shit. Wish I coulda caught them damn dogs. That chair's worth coupla grand."

"Yeah, and is probably somewhere past Yonkers by now."

chapter seventeen

The bullet that hit Flyin' Home in the armpit had pierced his lung, and while he was being prepped in the emergency room, he choked to death on his blood.

I sat at the table the next morning reading the *Daily Challenge,* which said it had been a drug hit. A drive-by. Even TooHot had warned me, in so many words, to stay away.

Flyin' Home had been dealing from his wheel-chair—traded one poor career choice for another.

I wondered if his girlfriend or wife or family had known. Had they ever tried to talk to him, warn him. Or would they now simply use some of his drug profits to bury him. And keep on stepping. I closed the paper, my feelings shifting from sympathy to anger and frustration and back again.

The only possible witness was now gone, and I

had a vision of Kendrick lying in his cell holding his ears against the sound of his nightmares.

Plus there was a new complication: *"If they seen me, they seen you too, you know what I'm sayin'?"* Flyin' Home had said.

I thought back to the night he had rolled up to me at Bert's place. There had been no cars on the avenue but who had been on the side streets? And he did get in the wind pretty fast, probably zigzagging through the blocks against the traffic pattern until he made it home.

Then last night, while talking to me, someone had caught up to him.

"If it was anybody but you, I wouldn't be here."

I shook my head. He'd be alive if he'd been home—or somewhere other than in that park.

The next day, when Teddi called, I had not been out of the house except to walk Ruffin. The image of Flyin' Home being lifted into the ambulance and the news of his death still haunted me.

I picked up the phone and Teddi's voice was barely above a whisper. I had to strain to hear her.

"Mali? Can you meet me at the theater? I've got to talk to you."

"What about?" I asked, not feeling in the mood to go anywhere but back to bed.

"Something's happened."

I didn't respond, not sure I was ready to absorb any more bad news.

"Mali, are you there?"

"I'm here. What . . . happened?"

"I can't say . . . can't talk about this over the phone. Can you meet me?"

I heard something more than the urgency in her voice, and I agreed to meet her. I dressed quickly and left the house.

Someone had placed a brighter bulb in the lobby of the Star Manhattan Theater and the cracks in the walls were visible. I climbed the stairs and expected to find a rehearsal in progress like the last time, but the only sound in the place came from the echo of my footfalls as I moved down the aisle.

The klieg lights were out but a small overhead bulb in center stage spread a weak glow. I stepped up on the stage and tried to peer into the darkness beyond the bulb.

"Teddi?"

I called again, wondering if she had changed her mind after she had phoned me. Maybe she was backstage and didn't hear me. I took a step, and a voice close to my ear made me jump.

"Mali . . ."

I spun around and Teddi was standing in the shadow of one of the sliding prop walls.

"I'm sorry, Mali. I didn't mean to frighten you, but I heard footsteps and I wasn't sure who it was . . ."

"Who else are you expecting?"

"No one. No one."

She stepped quickly off the stage and motioned for me to follow. We sat in the first row, where she positioned herself so that she could watch the door. I also glanced back but no one was there. "What's going on, Teddi?"

"Mali, I'm going to make this quick. I want you to forget about what I asked you to do. Right now, I'll give you half of what I offered and we'll call it even, okay?"

"No. No, it's not okay. I'm not talking about the money. I want to know why you wanted me to look into Thea's life in the first place, and now all of a sudden you're ready to fold."

"Please Mali . . . it's gotten too complicated. I don't want any more . . . I mean I think we should let sleeping dogs lie."

Sleeping dogs. Dogs. I thought of Flyin' Home. "You know," I said, "the only possible witness to Thea's murder was killed last night."

In what little light there was, I thought I saw the color drain from her face. She took a breath and pushed her hair back. The silence stretched before she spoke again.

"Mali, you're Kendrick's friend. I don't want anything to happen to anyone else. There's already too much—"

We both heard the sound of the door scraping open but I didn't move.

"Get down! Quick!" she whispered as she stood up and moved toward the sliver of light. "If she sees me talking to you . . ."

I slid down off my seat and crouched on the floor as she hurried up the aisle and stopped at the door.

"Mother? What are you doing here? There's no rehearsal today."

"I know. I phoned you, and when I didn't get an answer I thought—"

"Well, I was going over a script, but I'll get my bag. I was about to leave. Wait here."

Teddi moved back down the aisle and shot a quick look at me. I remained where I was as she rushed past me again. The sliver of light vanished as the door closed, leaving me in relative darkness and more confusion.

One day and several phone calls that Teddi did not return later, I looked at the other cards in the file.

I called Miss Adele, who was glad to hear from me. An hour later, I headed uptown to Esplanade Gardens, a co-op development that stretched in an L shape from Lenox Avenue and 146th Street to Seventh Avenue and 148th Street.

Across from Esplanade are the Dunbar Apartments, a block-long complex with interior gardens where Matthew Henson, Paul Robeson, W. E. B. Du Bois, Bill "Bojangles" Robinson, and A. Philip Randolph once lived. Miss Adele had also lived there for many years, but had moved across Seventh Avenue when Esplanade was completed.

One Christmastime when I was growing up, I went to Rockefeller Center for the tree-lighting cere-

mony, but every year after that I walked up Seventh
Avenue to Esplanade to watch the terraces come alive
with light so stunningly bright that Soviet cosmonauts
on a flyby recorded it as a pulse from a supernova. And
in a way, it was.

Each evening a week before Christmas, I would
rush uptown in freezing, sleeting, snowy weather to
stand in the entrance of Thelma's Lounge on the corner
of 148th Street and Seventh Avenue. I was too young to
enter the bar, so I would stand in the doorway blowing
rings of arctic air as lights from the terraces and windows across the avenue randomly pushed back the
frigid darkness. When I could no longer feel my mouth
move or my teeth chatter, I would board the bus and
head home. Those lights, the wonder and beauty of
them, were more exciting than any Christmas present I
had ever received.

I still walked uptown with Alvin and Ruffin occa-
sionally, and the lights at holiday time, now more subdued, still fascinated me.

Miss Adele's apartment looked out on Seventh Avenue
and faced her old apartment in the Dunbar. I took the
elevator to the eleventh floor, and when she opened the
door I could tell the AC wasn't on, but the apartment
seemed cool anyway. She wore a billowing yellow caftan
and her chestnut-colored braids were piled like a crown
on her head. She was barefoot, so I took off my shoes
and left them in the foyer. Pale beige carpeting

stretched wall-to-wall in every room except the kitchen, which had terra-cotta tile.

Just like Dad, she had a grand piano in the living room and artwork covering her walls. Her terrace was enclosed, converted into a small greenhouse with two wicker chairs squeezed in among dozens of plants.

I settled myself onto the deep sofa as she called from the kitchen. "How's your father? You should've brought him along. He works too hard, you know. Could use a break."

She came back into the living room and placed a tray of sandwiches and coffee on the low table, then sank comfortably onto the chair facing me. "Now what's this about Thea? Something else going on besides what the papers are saying?"

"I think so, but I'm not sure what to make of it," I said. "She was once involved with Kendrick Owen, the man who's in jail for her murder."

"But you don't think he did it?"

"No, I don't. I think the cops rushed to judgment, as usual, and tagged the most convenient person. But someone, a young man, told me that he saw a person leave the alley that night."

"Why doesn't he come forward?"

I showed her the article in the *Daily Challenge*. "He was killed three nights ago in a drive-by. I was two feet away from him."

Miss Adele read the paper, then put it down. "My God! This is terrible. What's going to happen to Kendrick?"

"I don't know. I'm back to square one. The only

thing left now is to look at Thea's life and figure out who would've wanted her dead."

I reached into my bag and knew I was taking a chance pulling out the bankbook and the photograph of the old woman. But Miss Adele had known my father since before I was born; she knew my mother. And she had been Thea's coach, the only one who'd cared enough to sponsor her dream of becoming somebody. I had to take the chance or forget everything.

Miss Adele looked at the picture and smiled, but when she opened the bankbook, I watched her brows come together.

"Poor Thea. Poor girl, poor thing . . ."

I waited, trying to drum up sympathy for a woman who had impacted so many lives I needed a scorecard to keep track. I thought of Laws, Kendrick, Roger, and Michaels: one dead, one in jail, one who'd been held hostage by a divorce settlement, and one whose political career might yet be compromised. Each, at one time or another, had been drawn to her.

It occurred to me that Thea's problem went a little beyond Lettie's syndrome. It was not what Thea had, but what she had wanted, wanted so badly that any one of these men—as much as they loved her—might've been better off with her dead.

Miss Adele spoke, cutting into my thoughts.

"That girl never got to enjoy anything. Never really got to live."

"But why not? I don't understand," I said.

She didn't answer, but closed the book and tapped

it thoughtfully against her open palm. "What're you going to do with this?"

"I don't know. Actually, I'm not even supposed to have it."

"How'd you get it?"

"Well, I didn't steal it, if that's what you're asking. I was helping Gladys Winston sort through Thea's stuff. I found it in the apartment in a place where no one but Thea would've known where it was."

That seemed to satisfy her, and I calmed down, allowing my defensiveness to fade.

She glanced at the book again, leafing through the pages. "Do you have any idea, Mali, where the money came from? Who made these deposits?"

I shrugged. "Maybe one of her boyfriends. I don't know which one."

She put the bankbook on the table and reached for her cup. Her fingers were fine and long and seamless, as if age had skipped over them and went directly to her wrists, with their prominent veins. She took a sip but still did not look at me.

"Michaels, perhaps?"

"You know about Michaels?" I asked.

"Who doesn't? Anyone in Harlem with half an eye could see what was happening. Even his wife."

"Do you think Anne might've . . . ?"

"No. She's too . . . refined for that."

"Sometimes refinement can take a backseat when your last nerve is plucked," I said, remembering how Anne had treated Rita Bayne that day at the beauty salon.

Miss Adele looked at me, frowning at my lack of sympathy. "This is rather complicated, Mali." I was about to apologize, but she continued. "But then, Thea had a complicated history, poor thing."

I had to bite my tongue. If I heard that "poor thing" tag one more time I would throw up.

"How so?" I managed to ask.

"Well, this woman," Miss Adele took the small photograph from the table and cupped it in the palm of her hand, like a jewel. "This is Dessie Hamilton. Thea's grandmother."

I nodded. "Dad said that Dessie had worked in the Half-Moon years ago."

Miss Adele placed the picture on the table again and gazed at it as if she expected the face in the photo to speak.

"Dessie," she murmured, more to the picture than to me, "was so beautiful it made you smile just to look at her. I don't know if your father told you that she had been a dancer at the Cotton Club. She was some beauty, even though she danced in the back row.

"The gangsters decided her legs weren't that shapely, so they put her in back of the big-leg dancers. But that didn't matter. She had some hips and knew what to do with them—like Josephine Baker. And those men caught a glimpse of her and stayed till closing.

"A few of the girls—not all of them—had 'friends,' as we liked to call them in those days. But Dessie held out for the richest one. She figured if it was gonna happen, let it be worth her while. The man was in oil and kept her in furs for twenty years. Except that he was jealous. She couldn't go anywhere, not that she wanted to, 'cause she loved him. He didn't want her dancing anymore, so she quit. And they were quite a pair. Went to the Broadway shows, the opera, the night-clubs. She had a beautiful apartment and a maid to clean it. She never had to cook."

I nodded, wondering if this was in the genes: Thea's lifestyle passed down to her the way my mother had given me my gray eyes. "So Dessie's life was some-thing out of a fairy *tale*?"

"Almost. Except who knows how those things end sometimes? The man died suddenly and didn't leave her much, just some bearer bonds. And she found out she was pregnant. So she got rid of her Cadillac and her furs one by one, and then the bonds."

She glanced at me, then stared until my unsympa-thetic gaze wavered and fell away.

"I know what you're thinking, Mali, but you must remember the times. We're talking early forties. Dessie had stayed home for years. She wasn't prepared or trained to work. And what options did black women have back then? The most practical one was to stand at 163rd Street on Grand Concourse in the Bronx in a crowd, and if you got lucky some white woman drove up and picked you up to do hours of backbreaking housework and at the end of the day put two dollars in your hand after deducting for a lunch sandwich so stale your own dog wouldn't have eaten it.

"But Dessie didn't go that way; learned quick

enough to pinch a penny so hard old Abe cried. That kept her together until the baby was almost two years old. Then one day, she was pushing the carriage down Seventh Avenue and passed the Half-Moon Bar, and the owner, who knew the whole story, offered her a job.

"At that time, it was mostly men behind those counters, but he put Dessie in there and business boomed. Dessie stayed even during the war, when she could've made more money in a defense plant, but she'd heard those stories about how the best jobs went to all the white folks first—even the old, crippled ones—before they would hire the blacks, and she said no thanks, she'd had her share of short change from white folks. Besides, money was flowing in Harlem in those days. The Moon was jumping and she jumped right with it.

"She made enough to send her daughter to boarding school, a white boarding school, because she wanted that child to have the education and advantages she herself didn't have. Besides, the child, Marcella, looked white enough, so why not act white and be white.

"Marcella came home most holidays, but sometimes she visited or went home with her rich classmates. God knows the grand tale she must've concocted to keep that lie going.

"When Marcella graduated, Dessie went. I don't know how she pulled that off. I mean Dessie was pretty pale herself, with straight hair, but . . . not enough to be *white*-white. Must've said she was Mediterranean or the maid or something. I don't know. Anyway, we spent the next six months laughing about it."

"Was it that funny?" I asked.

Miss Adele fixed me with a stare, and from her silence I came to understand that it wasn't real laughter at all but the sounds we make to keep from crying, what we do when we realize race has poisoned the core of this country, and the sound we make is the distraction that keeps us from killing somebody.

"So I laugh," Miss Adele said, "when I hear white folks say they can trace their family to some village in Scotland or back to France at the time of Louis the Fourteenth. Fine, I say. Except they conveniently blank out that period of slavery when African women were having as many babies by white owners as they were by African men. A lot of those owners sent those white-looking children to Europe to live, marry, and have European children whose grandmama was black.

"Other children, who were sold away because the owners didn't want to be reminded, faded into the larger population, their blackness bleached, in the chaos of the Civil War. So I smile because somewhere in the murk of miscegenation is the true legacy that this country refuses to address."

"So what Dessie did with her daughter," I said, "sending her away to a different life, wasn't new. She was just following a certain pattern."

"I suppose, but it seemed to me like too damned much work, and I told Dessie so. I mean the bottom line is we really don't know anyone's true pedigree.

Anyway, Marcella went away to college, and the summer before she was to graduate, she came home with a baby."

"Thea?"

"Thea. Yes."

"Was her father black or white?"

"Who knows? Marcella stayed exactly one day, stepped out to get something from the store, and never came back. A month later, Dessie received a letter from Nevada, saying Marcella was all right. Later, we heard that she'd been killed in an auto accident on the West Coast."

"So Dessie raised Thea?"

"Yes. Thea never knew her mother or her father."

"Did she ever ask?"

"I suppose so. What child isn't going to ask about her parents. But how're you gonna dig up the dead? Marcella was gone. Nothing you could do about that, can you?"

I sat back, cradling my cup in my hand, thinking how we're all affected by death in different ways. I knew how I felt about Benin at times, but I couldn't remember my grief spilling over into such a state where I wandered like a catatonic through everything, allowing everyone to do for me, care for me, touch me, and yet feel nothing.

But at times, Thea had indeed felt *something*. Anger, perhaps. Or jealousy. Probably had been jealous of Gladys and her close family. And she'd showed major attitude toward me when Dad had introduced us at the club.

Miss Adele leaned forward and picked up Dessie's picture again. "When all this is straightened out and if this picture is available, I'd like to have it," she said.

"I'll see what I can do," I said.

"What do you intend to do with the bankbook?"

"What is there to do," I said, "but get it back where it belongs as fast as possible."

chapter eighteen

By the time I left Miss Adele, the rain that had been falling had stopped and a late-afternoon sun was edging out of the scattering clouds to bathe Seventh Avenue in a pale coral glow. The wind was cool and smelled faintly of fresh wet leaves. I cut over to Lenox Avenue, where folks with TGIF tattooed on their foreheads emerged from the subway at 145th Street, rushing home in order to rush back out.

Friday-evening party energy was in the air and I needed to catch up with Gladys before she left her office. I dialed her number and one of the brokers answered. "Miss Winston is with a client," she said when I gave her my name. "Mali Anderson? Wait, just a minute."

Gladys came on. "Mali. How're you doing?" Her tone was edged with impatience.

"Sorry to bother you," I said. "I wanted to know when we're going back to Thea's."

"Probably next week. I haven't had time. I'll call you."

She hung up abruptly and I felt relieved. She'd probably been too busy to go back to the apartment.

I walked down Lenox to 143rd Street, where two large oil-drum shaped barbecue stoves near the curb broadcast a smoking, sharp hickory fragrance into the air. The stoves belonged to Old Man Charleston, and the waiting buyers stepped back as he ambled out of the tiny take-out restaurant draped in a chef's toque and glistening white apron.

He cut through the crowd like an ocean liner and opened the stoves to coat the meat with a spread of Charleston's secret sauce. I watched and wondered, as I often did, where the secret came from, since Charleston had been born right down the avenue in Harlem Hospital.

After serving a stretch for burglary in the sixties, he'd come out and flipped burgers in a 42nd-Street greasy spoon until his parole was up, then started his street barbecue with a charcoal stove and an umbrella stand. In a year he'd made enough to lease a sliver of store so narrow that CHARLESTON had to be printed vertically on the window.

He cooked ribs and chicken outdoors summer and winter, and paid his fines promptly when he was ticketed. The take-out line grew longer by the season and often included some of the same cops who ticketed him.

"Fifteen more minutes," he announced and wiped his dark face with the plaid towel suspended from his back pocket. "Good things come to those who wait," he reminded the few grumblers before he disappeared back into the store.

I followed him inside and he smiled when he saw me. "Mali, Baby. Long time no see. Whassup?"

"Nothing and plenty." I laughed. "I need an order of ribs and a favor."

"The ribs you got. Name the favor."

"I need your picks."

"Locked out again?"

"Again," I said. He reached under the counter and pulled a palm-size case from the shelf.

"Mali, I can see in your face you ain't locked out this time, but don't tell me what you want 'em for. I don't want to know. Just have 'em back here tomorrow A.M."

"What're you doing? Renting them out?"

He raised his hands and stepped back. "Mali, I'm *shocked. Shocked* that you—"

"Come on, Charleston. Are you?"

"Hell no. I may *look* like a fool but that's as far as it go. Suppose I rent some dude these picks, he lends 'em to a crackhead, and I go home and find my own crib cleaned. Do that make sense? Only reason I want 'em back here is so I'll know where they are."

I folded my elbows on the narrow counter. "I've been meaning to ask you why you keep them."

"Girl, sometimes you ask the damnedest questions." He opened a stack of plastic containers and inspected them for flaws.

"Listen, I keep 'em to look at every now and then. Specially when things git a little tight, what with the rent and all the other bills, you know what I'm sayin'? I pull this box out and gaze long and hard at my used-to-be life. Everybody has somethin' they don't never want to go back to. Me, I'll take the cradle—die—before I see the slammer again. I keep this box to remind me how I got there and to let me know that no matter how bad things are, they ain't never gonna git as tough as it was in the joint."

As he talked, he filled a take-out carton with coleslaw, red rice, and yams, and left enough space for the ribs. He moved quickly and I marveled how someone so large was able to maneuver in such a small space: like the night I wanted a rib sandwich and walked in on the two stickup men who had him pressed to the wall.

I had been on the job then, and when I'd yelled "Freeze! Police!" Charleston slid out of sight so fast behind the counter I thought the wall he'd been leaning against had been oiled.

I had drawn my weapon and called for backup when one perp broke for the door. Charleston sprang up with a short-handled chopping knife—the kind you see being flipped in those Benihana restaurants—except that Charleston's had something extra. Speed. The knife flew past me in a triple arc before landing in the perp's shoulder blade. A witness later said the momentum pushed the guy down Lenox and right on through the revolving door of Harlem Hospital.

I would stop in on Charleston from time to time after that, but it wasn't until I'd left the department that we became good friends. I had come home from a party one night and found I had lost my keys. Dad was playing a wedding upstate and Alvin was sleeping over at a friend's.

Ruffin was smart, but not smart enough to unlock the door. Plus, when he heard my voice, he'd set up a howl so loud I thought someone had died. So I went to Charleston's to sit over coffee and a doughnut until Dad got home.

The coffee was so bad it talked back. I told Charleston so and he leaned on the counter.

"I see your mind went the way of your keys, but don't come jumpin' in my face. I didn't make you lose 'em. Anyway," he'd said, reaching under the counter, "take these and try 'em. See what happens. Bring 'em back first thing in the A.M."

He'd opened the set and showed me how to use them. When I returned them the next day, I said, "You didn't have to do this for me, especially after I talked wrong about your coffee."

"Well, that's why I had to git you outta here," he'd said. "My coffee's bad, but it's the best in the neighborhood. You was makin' me look shaky." He winked and laughed and we'd been friends ever since.

Now he slid the case across the counter. "A.M., okay?"

"No problem, Charleston. A.M."

My nerves got the better of me, and before I reached 116th Street I donated my dinner to a street person. It wouldn't do to have Charleston's secret sauce lingering in Thea's elegant apartment, even though she was no longer there.

At Graham Court the wrought-iron gates were locked, but I hung around long enough to walk through with several people returning home. Some had stepped off the bus with large packages and others were pushing shopping carts. An older woman paused at the entrance of Thea's building and I helped lift her cart and carry it inside.

I smiled and chatted until she rolled the cart off on the third floor. On the eighth floor, I stepped off. I looked around the empty hallway and it was so quiet I could hear my breath rushing in and out. My chest was tight and I wanted to move fast. Get in and get out again.

I rang the bell first, just in case, then selected the first pick in the box. It went in easily and I pressed my ear to the lock, listening, as Charleston had said, for the tumblers to fall in place. I inserted a second pick below the first one and eased it back and forth until I heard the click, then pushed against the door and it opened.

I made my way down the foyer and through the living room without turning on the lights, even though the daylight had faded. I went straight to the bedroom and felt for the zipper behind the headboard.

Don't sit on the bed. Don't leave any telltale impression. My fingers were damp as I opened the zipper and slipped the bankbook and photo back inside. The sweat was running down my arm. I also needed to go to the bathroom, but in the dark my nervousness was getting in my way.

Don't go to the bathroom. Just get the hell on out.
Even if you have to pee on yourself in the elevator. Get out.

I paused near the foot of the bed, trying to remember if the door had a slam lock or if I had to fumble with the picks again. Charleston hadn't mentioned that part. I was about to step into the living room when I heard a sound and saw a sliver of light. Someone had opened the door and was coming down the hall.

I backed into the bedroom, quietly sank to my knees, and slid on my stomach under the bed. The sound of the footsteps lessened but a light crunching still told me the person was walking silently across the thick carpet in the living room. The crunch came nearer and stopped at the foot of the bed. A click sounded and a small white circle swept along the floor, then arced up and disappeared.

I lay still as the mattress above me made a soft groan. The zipper sounded almost rusty as it opened and closed. And I held my breath as the flashlight fell to the floor and the circle of light shone directly into my face. Before the flashlight could roll under the bed, a hand scooped it up, clicked it off, and the person left the room.

I heard the front door close but waited several minutes before I rolled out from under the bed and tiptoed to the bathroom.

I was debating whether to flush the toilet when I heard the sound again.

It can't be! Another key? Is someone else coming in? The place had more damn traffic than Penn Station. Why can't they let the dead rest in peace?

The door closed quietly and the same footsteps—I was sure it was the same person—were now moving quickly toward the bathroom. I jumped away from the door and stepped into the tub behind the heavy shower curtain.

It was a man who flipped the lid and muttered under his breath at the unflushed toilet.

I held my breath and crouched low like a runner, feeling the cold porcelain against one knee and the palms of my hands.

. . . If he opens this curtain.

. . . *If he opens the curtain, girl, don't let him catch you praying. Do what you gotta do!* The whisper was strong, yet calm. It faded then whispered again: *Use what's at hand.*

I didn't smile but now I was ready to spring up like a cat, knowing that my weight and his surprise would be enough to knock him off his feet. I didn't need to go a Tyson ten, just one fast fist to his face would be all I needed to get me in the wind. I crouched lower and felt the sweat curl down my arms.

Steady, Mali. Steady . . .

The footsteps walked slowly past the tub, the light went off, and the bathroom door closed.

I remained still for several minutes, until my knee started to complain. Finally, I eased up and was about to step out of the tub when one curtain was suddenly snatched back. In the dark, I grabbed the other curtain—they were heavy damask designer numbers—and vaulted out against the man, heaving the curtain over his head and arms.

"My God! What the hell—? Who the hell—?"

I managed to knock the breath out of him as we fell to the floor and he hit his head on the tile. By the time I'd sprinted to the door, he was groaning, trying to stagger to his feet.

Outside in the hallway, I ran for the stairs and was through the courtyard and out in the street in the time it took to dial 911. If indeed he dialed 911. Whoever it was probably did not belong there any more than I did. That's why the lights were out.

I walked fast down 116th Street without looking back and lost myself in the crowd of Lenox Avenue.

Dad came up from his study when I walked in. "Alvin called just five minutes ago. Still having a good time and doesn't want to come home. But I told him he has to be home by the last week in August. Boy needs time to wind down before thinking about school." He paused. "You look kinda out of it. What's wrong?"

"Nothing that a dry martini wouldn't fix."

He went to the bar, fixed two drinks, and handed me one. I tried not to show my nervousness. "I'll be glad when he comes home," I said, not sounding too convincing. The time will fly by and Kendrick will probably still be in jail. I had no idea, no plan about what to do next. Suddenly I felt too tired to enjoy my drink. I put the glass down and was about to retreat to my room, when Dad said, "So, how's Adele?"

I picked up the glass again and settled in on the sofa. "She's fine," I said. "Talked a bit about Thea, but mostly about Dessie. I didn't know Dessie was Thea's grandmother. Or that she'd once danced at the Cotton Club."

He lifted his glass and took a swallow before he answered, "Yep."

"Did you know Dessie?"

"Slightly."

"How come you never mentioned it."

" 'Cause you never asked."

"Come on, Dad. What's up?"

Another minute passed before he made up his mind. Finally he said, "Story is Dessie was an original Cotton Club Cutie whose bills had been paid by her downtown daddy, and when he closed his eyes without mentioning her in his will, she'd had to sell her silver Cadillac and get a real job. Finally ended up on the other side of that knife-scarred counter of the Half-Moon serving two-for-one shots of watered vodka for the next forty-three years. But I never mentioned her."

"Why not?"

He moved to the bar and mixed another drink and then leaned over to refill my glass. When he spoke again, his voice was low and his speech deliberate.

"Did you know that your mother's mother had wanted to be a dancer too? When she came to New York as a young girl, her head was filled with all the tales about Harlem and all the fabulous places. She'd heard about Connie's Inn, the Club Sudan, Smalls' Paradise, but most of all she wanted to dance at the Cotton Club. Dance was going to be her life. Here was a young girl who could out-strut anything on two legs. And she was beautiful.

"One day she walked into that club, and not un-derstanding the stares and snickers, asked for a job. The gangsters didn't even let her try out. They looked at one another, and at her skin, and then offered her a job cleaning the ladies' room. One told her she might even be too dark for that.

"She walked out and never danced again. Not even at the Savoy. She eventually finished school and became a teacher. But the Cotton Club? That name was never mentioned in her house. When your mother was growing up, she had to promise to complete her educa-tion first before she got serious about a dance career.

"Dessie was a good dancer, so I heard. That's all I can say because that's all I know. As far as I'm con-cerned, the less said about the old Cotton Club, the better."

I finished my drink in silence, understanding that this talk would not happen again. I hadn't seen my father so sad and angry in a long time.

When he left, I changed into fresh jeans and a T-shirt and went around to Charleston's to return the picks.

"You finished fast," he said when I walked in. "And look like you peeped in somebody's grave."

"Not quite," I said. I leaned against the counter, wanting to fold my arms and rest my head.

"I need two orders of ribs with extra everything and extra sauce," I finally said.

He took two large containers from the overhead

shelf, glanced at me again, and then pointed to the sign next to the one that read:

CREDIT DIED YESTERDAY SO DON'T ASK FOR HIM.

A smaller sign read:

THERE'S NOTHING LIKE TRUE LOVE
BUT MY RIBS WILL HOLD YOU TILL YOU FIND IT.

He tapped the smaller sign. "Mali, three orders in one day ain't good, Honey. Even if it *is* my food. What's goin' on with you?"

"Nothing I can't handle. Besides, one of these is for my hairdresser."

Now he really stared at me—and at my afro, which had probably shrunk from the sweat of my earlier encounter and was now plastered against my scalp like tight little pea pods.

"Your hairdresser. Mm-hmm. When was the last time you was there?"

"Please, Charleston, you wouldn't understand."

"Try me."

"Not tonight. I'm too tired."

He packed the orders and I paid him and walked over to Eighth Avenue. It was nearly ten o'clock but the lights were still on and Bertha was working on a customer. Before she said hello, she said, "You brought me something from Charleston."

She moved away from the woman in the chair and came over to inspect the bag. "Damn, this smells good.

You know how he got his name? Years ago, he was on the lam for six months and got tagged in Charleston for walkin' against the light. Ain't that somethin'. Gettin' tripped over a little thing like that."

Bert turned to the woman and put the last curls in place, misted her hair with spray sheen, and handed her a mirror. The woman gazed without comment, paid her bill, and left.

Bert counted the money and sighed.

"Not even a nickel tip. I was just about to close when she stepped in claimin' she had a hot date. I shoulda flipped the sign in her face."

She flipped the CLOSED sign now and opened the package.

"Ain't seen you in a few days, Mali."

"No. I've been trying to figure out what to do now that Flyin' Home is dead. He was the one who could've helped Kendrick."

"Maybe," Bert said, spreading her napkin in her lap, "you oughtta go back and look at Thea again."

"Last time I looked, she was dead also," I said.

"I mean, look again at her life."

"Or look around it. I had a short meeting with Teddi Lovette yesterday."

"What happened?"

"Nothing. Early on, she had wanted to find out stuff about Thea also. Then yesterday she calls me downtown to the theater to ask me to forget the whole deal. I think the woman has some mental problems and so does her mama."

Bert did not answer and we ate in silence. Then she shook her head.

"I think," she said, eyeing her forkful of collards as if she expected to find a worm sautéed among the green, "I think Kendrick finally told her."

"Told her what?"

"That he wasn't interested in her. That's probably why she wants you to back off now."

chapter nineteen

ith all the other stuff happening, I'd had no time to think about Dr. Thomas's party. On Wednesday morning, I sat at the breakfast table staring at the money near my plate, wondering if it was a mirage. Then I looked at Dad again.

"Do you mean it?"

"Of course. Consider it a bonus."

"But three hundred dollars to buy a dress. I—"

"I want you to wear something decent this evening. You know how Blaine Thomas is. He likes everything just so, especially his guests."

"But I'm not a guest. I'm his neighbor. We're his neighbors, his friends."

"Mali, this is a political fund-raiser and this friend'll be in a dinner jacket and this friend doesn't want to see his daughter in that threadbare black dress."

Threadbare. My little black dress. What could I say. I was too shocked to be angry and had too little time to drool over my windfall. It was 10 A.M. The party was scheduled for 7 P.M. I sailed out the door and forty-five minutes later was standing in front of a full-length mirror in Gourd Chips, an Afrocentric clothing shop on Court Street in Brooklyn. The black-and-white hand-painted design on a flared cotton jacket and wrap pants beckoned as soon as I stepped through the door. "I'll take it," I said, turning a final time.

Then I doubled back to Mart 125 for a pair of sterling-silver hoops I had salivated over for two months. By 5 P.M. I was home, lying across the bed, my eyelids draped with fresh cucumber slices, and Stevie Wonder's *Songs in the Key of Life* flowing softly in the background.

I lay there thinking about Anne Michaels and what she'd be wearing. I also thought about Rita, the senator's assistant. I wondered, with her new hairstyle, if she would have the same rhinestone glasses she'd worn in the Pink Fingernail.

Dr. Thomas lived two doors away, and it was five after seven when I rang the bell, congratulating myself for being early. The door opened and already present was that small fanatic band who had dedicated themselves to stamping out the last vestiges of CPT (colored people's time, where one arrived so late the guests were already leaving).

I smiled, imagining them poised at the sound of the starter's pistol, then charging down the block to ring the bell at exactly Seven Pee-em on the Dot. They were the folks who took all the fun out of "arriving."

One did not walk through the door of Blaine Thomas's house so much as one *arrived*—the way movie stars did it in those grainy black-and-white thirties fantasies: pausing in grand foyers to deposit pearl-handled walking sticks, Dracula-inspired capes, furs, and other necessary accessories into the arms of faceless factotums.

There was no thirties drama tonight. The only hired help were the lone brass-buttoned bartender standing at parade rest behind a mahogany bar stacked with an impressive pyramid of liquor and a chef from Copeland's Catering carefully adding the finishing touches to an exquisite buffet.

So one arrived in the foyer with its gallery of art and moved on to the double parlor with its bleached-oak spiral staircase and a glass table where the political factotums waited to accept the checks necessary for Senator Michaels's campaign.

Dr. Thomas had a large psychiatric practice and he had helped me through the difficult period following Benin's death. He and Dad had been friends for forty years, but I wasn't sure how long he'd known Edwin Michaels.

Dad's music drifted from the rear parlor, and I moved toward the sound. He sat at the piano, fingers floating over the keys.

"You look beautiful," he said.

I kissed him on the forehead. "Thanks, Dad."

"For what?"

"Foresight," I said, and moved back to the front

parlor. Mildred Thomas, small and elegant in a pleated
column of yellow silk, waved to me. At fifty-something
with round wire frames and close-cut hair, she looked
more like Dr. Thomas's daughter than his wife.

"You look gorgeous," she said, and I felt grateful
to Dad again.

The door opened and Mildred walked toward it,
pulling me along. When Rita stepped in, I scarcely recognized her.

"This is Rita Bayne, Senator Michaels's assistant."

"We met earlier, a week and a half ago in the
Pink Fingernail," I said, marveling at Miss Viv's handi-
work. Rita's hair was highlighted with auburn and
pinned away from her face, and her brows were brown
crescents above kohl-lined lids. She blinked rapidly and
I guessed that the rhinestone glasses had been left at
home and the contacts were something she was struggling to get used to. Her black knit dress downplayed
most of the usual structural defects, and a small black
crocheted bag hung from her left wrist.

"I remember you," she said. "I remember your
eyes. Unusual." She continued to blink, and I nodded
and smiled. And kept smiling, refusing to confirm if the
pale gray coloring was inherited from my mother or
bought from Bloomingdale's Optical.

"Come," said Mildred, escorting us to the bar,
where the waiter had the blender churning out a line of
piña coladas.

The bell rang and Mildred excused herself. Dad's
low-keyed notes floated just above the hum of conversation as more people arrived. I watched old friends pause

to admire additions to the Thomases' art collection and
newcomers move quickly to absorb everything twice in
their short visit.

Clusters of deal makers were forming, and the
high welcoming sounds dropped by degrees to confidential lows. The caterer stood by, ready with linen and
silver, but it was too early. The ritual patting of shoulders was only in the first round.

At the bar, there was a break in the froth of piña
coladas and the bartender looked disappointed when I
pointed at the Absolut.

"A cosmopolitan, please."

"Make that two," said Rita.

She glanced at the piña coladas and sighed. "You
know how many calories are in a quarter cup of coconut
milk?"

I had no idea but tried to imagine the willpower
one needed to consciously pass on something so wonderful and destructive. Tonight I wanted a variation of
martini containing a lot of vodka, a little Cointreau, and
dashes of cranberry and lime. The bartender was true to
his calling and mixed it without my asking twice.

"Miss Viv did a lovely job on your hair," I said,
looking for an opening.

"You really like it? I don't know. Somehow, this
isn't really me."

I wondered what she meant but didn't pursue it.
"How long have you worked for the senator?" I asked,
turning her attention away from the calories and the
uncomfortable new look. The black dress neutralized

the stocky build and allowed her to move among the crowd smiling and polite, but how did she manage at home, stepping out of the shower late at night when—like every one of us with defects real or imagined—she was susceptible to the mirror's uncompromising reality?

I knew how I felt about my feet, which had grown so fast when I was a kid I was convinced I'd never have to rent a pair of skis in my life. I glanced down. Rita may not have been centerfold material, but she had small feet.

A real martini is meant to be sipped slowly, during conversation breaks, or between long drags on long cigarettes. The drink is designed to outlast the cigarette, but no one was smoking and Rita had no gauge. Two minutes after it had been placed in her hand, she was staring at the bottom of her empty glass.

"How long have I worked for Edwin?" she finally responded, giving herself time to shape an answer. "Almost two years. He's a friend of the family. My parents thought it would be a good idea, this work I mean, to get me involved in . . . things. I never went out much, even in college. Sort of stayed to myself, stuck to the books and things. So this . . . exposure has been . . . good."

She was on edge and talking fast to fill up the space between words. She looked at her glass and was about to reorder when the doorbell rang again. Edwin Michaels strolled in, followed by his wife, who paused in the foyer to kiss Mildred Thomas on the cheek. Dr.

Thomas, who had been speaking to a man and a woman in the library, came forward.

"Well, Edwin, good to see you."

There was the wave and swell of peripheral activity as the two shook hands. Cameras flashed, and Dad pressed the keys, blowing the notes up to enlarge the occasion.

Voices rose, drinks were swallowed, and smiles got wider as the handshaking extended beyond the host to the check writers.

Edwin Michaels was a shade under six feet and remained standing on the bottom step leading into the parlor. This put him head and shoulders above everyone except Dr. Thomas, who was at least six three, but since no one expected a speech this early, he stepped into the room waving, smiling, reaching for more hands.

He was dressed impeccably in a dark blue suit, striped tie, and white shirt. His smile looked almost spontaneous and his teeth were whiter than I remembered.

I turned to Rita but she had stepped back to the bar and now held tightly to a second martini. Her expression had changed from unfocused blinking to a sad stare. I glanced quickly at Michaels but he had not seen her.

"Are you okay?" I whispered.

She did not answer and the bartender watched, thin-lipped, as she opened her mouth and drank as if she held a glass of water. When the glass was empty, she placed it on the bar.

"Excuse me," she murmured in my direction,

though I wasn't sure if she was speaking to me. "I have to . . . I have to find the bathroom."

I watched her move away from the crowd and into the hallway and wondered how long she'd been in love with Edwin Michaels.

chapter twenty

Edwin Michaels didn't have to work at being good-looking. He simply was. He had deep-set eyes, a full mouth, graying hair cut close against dark skin, and a slightly crooked, prominent nose that let you know that everything about him wasn't perfect. He was, in his own way, as handsome as Tad, but the difference between the two was attitude. Tad had none and Edwin couldn't show enough.

Dad took a break and a CD of Miles Davis's *Miles of Miles* filtered through the low hum. The circulating crowd kept the bartender busy. Anne Michaels, relaxed and in her element, leaned against the piano, talking with Dad. I decided to look for Rita. Maybe she'd passed out. Not everyone can handle a martini, at least not that fast.

Down the hall, the bathroom door was ajar. I cautiously pushed it open, expecting to find a body draped over the sink, but the room was empty. I peered into the library a few feet away, where a Tiffany floor lamp illuminated the bookshelves, lead-paned windows, a tall liquor cabinet near a leather sofa, a writing desk, and two small chairs.

I doubled back to the rear parlor and slipped through the French doors leading to the garden. The moon spilled dim spears of light over the area, but there was no one outside. Probably because the deals and connections were being made inside and no one wanted to miss a play.

The garden was an oasis. I remained very still, thinking of Benin and how we'd once played hide-and-seek in this calm and quiet place. I moved down the three steps and toward the fountain, which had been calibrated so that it didn't quite splash but sent a small cascade bubbling into a shallow blue-tiled pool.

On the bottom step, voices drifted toward me. Someone, a couple, was standing near the bench under the arbor-like enclosure formed by an overgrowth of rose of Sharon.

I recognized Rita's whisper, even with the slight slur.

"But I did this . . . for you. For you. And you promised—"

"I know what I promised, but—"

"But what? Edwin, listen to me. Please. I killed someone for nothing."

"He was sleaze. He deserved it."

"I killed him, Edwin. Just to get back that letter you were stupid enough to give to Thea. How could you acknowledge on paper that the baby was yours?

How could you? I saw Laws take it out of her purse that night at the bar. At first I thought it was money, thought he was stealing the money you might've given her, but the envelope was too flat—not unless it was a check again, but even with a check I knew you'd write a note. That's what love will do. But a whole long letter?"

"Rita, listen: You've been drinking. And it is not the time or the place for this kind of—"

"Yes I've had a drink. So what? You won't give me five minutes of your time anyplace else. Too busy. Always rushing through the office, brushing me aside. I don't exist. Except when you need me in bed."

"This party is supposed to be a fund-raiser, not a confessional, Rita."

"Don't patronize me. If I hadn't gotten that letter back, there'd be no more fund-raisers."

He looked at his watch, then glanced back toward the doors, which I had just moved away from. Apparently satisfied that everyone inside was preoccupied, he said, "You have five minutes, Rita."

"When Laws called the office, I was the one to pick up the phone. I was the one, Edwin."

"I know, Rita, I—"

"Do you? He intended to blackmail you, squeeze you dry and then give the letter to Dora Peterson's campaign people. You know what that would've done to you?"

"Rita, I appreciate—"

"I don't want your appreciation. I . . . killed someone for you. I want what you promised me." She paused before continuing. "You said you were tired of

Anne, tired of her freezing you every night. You liked the way I worked you in bed. You said so; I didn't imagine it. One time you even said I did more for you than Thea. Remember?"

I couldn't believe what I was hearing, and I bent lower and shifted toward the curve behind the wall of ivy. Thank God the childhood hiding place was still there, and had been made even more obscure by the growth of English ivy suspended from the balcony above. I pressed into its shadow and parted the cascade of vines to peep out.

Edwin had her in his arms now, tipping her chin and kissing her. "Rita, you're a beautiful woman. I made a promise to you. Thea's gone so don't think about her any longer. What happened, what I felt for her, was a kind of fever. I was crazy, couldn't think straight. But she's gone now and—"

"But you still think of her."

The soft desperation in Rita's voice was so profound it washed over me, shaking me like a wave.

Edwin's voice came again, easy and soothing, barely above a whisper. "Of course I still think about her. It takes time to come down . . . from a thing like that."

"But you were screwing me," Rita interrupted, "every spare minute. Even when she was alive . . ."

"Listen." He touched her hair, pushing a strand behind her ear. "I can tell you this: When the campaign's over, we're going to sit down and make plans. But we've got to do it right. Make the least waves, you hear me? I love you. You're beautiful and I love you."

"Oh, Edwin."

"Now: Where'd you put the letter? I've been asking you for a few days now."

"And I told you: It's in a safe place."

"I know, Sweetheart, I know." He ran his hands down the small of her back and nuzzled her ear. "You're good at keeping me safe. You're really good. But I—"

"Please, Edwin—"

"I thought you said you loved me. Love means trust, Beautiful. Do you love me?"

"Do I—? How can you ask me that? When Laws called, do you know what it took for me to go back to that bar? At three in the morning on a rainy night when no one was in the street? I didn't even take a cab. I walked. Laws was just about to close."

Rita's voice trailed off and I watched her step away and stand near the bench. A minute passed before she spoke again.

"We went into his office and . . . and . . . you know what he wanted me to do . . . to him. I had the money but he said he wanted a bonus."

"Oh, Rita, Baby. I—"

"He counted the five thousand dollars and he smiled. Then he went to the desk and pulled the letter out. 'You know what this is worth?' he said. 'Five thousand and a blow is cheap, too cheap. You talking about a man's career, serious business!'

"He opened the desk again and pulled out a pack of condoms. A whole pack—as if he expected to make a night of it.

"The letter was on the desk and we both stared at it. Then he heard a sound, like someone was trying the front door, even though most of the lights were out. Laws peeped through the blinds, then turned away from me to put the condom on. That's when I snatched the letter opener from the desk.

"I got him in the neck and he was choking and coughing and he fell and I guess I could've stopped there. But something—someone else was holding that blade tight in my hand. I couldn't think. I couldn't stop . . ."

Her voice trailed away and she sat down, holding her head in her hands. "Edwin, I just couldn't . . . stop."

In the moonlight, she looked as if she had retracted into herself like a turtle. A chill came over me and I held my hands to my mouth to keep from calling out. *Don't tell him. Don't tell him where that letter is!*

I bit the inside of my mouth and held my breath, listening to the faint trickle of the fountain. Edwin stepped from the arbor and looked down at Rita. She was still sitting on the bench, bent over, her hands to her face. He did not touch her. Instead he straightened his tie and glanced again toward the steps. When he spoke, his voice was still low, but almost normal, and I didn't have to strain to make out his words.

"Listen, Rita: In a week or so, I expect to get my hands on some money, several thousand dollars, in fact. I'll send you to St. Thomas until this blows over."

"Campaign money?" she said, looking up. Her

voice wavered. "You're using money you don't even have yet."

"It's not campaign money. It's one hundred thousand from someone else. Half of it's yours if you go to St. Thomas."

I watched her shake her head. "I will never go to that place again. After what you did the last time, never."

"Well, we'll talk about that later. Right now I have to get back inside. People'll begin to wonder what happened to me. You know how to wait a few minutes before coming in. And don't drink anything else. You've had too much already."

He turned away and left her sitting there, bent over again, with her face in her hands.

I pressed farther into the ivy until my back was against the wall. I did not breathe. He passed me and I could have reached out and tapped his shoulder. Or hit him in the head if I'd had a baseball bat. His cologne, a subtle expensive fragrance, lingered in the air, and his gaze focused straight ahead, entirely without expression.

He climbed the three steps and disappeared inside. I knew he would not look back and I stepped out of my niche before Rita moved her hands from her face. She was still crying and I wanted to go to her but I couldn't. She'd know I'd been here the whole time. I thought of sneaking up the steps, waiting one minute, then coming back out as if nothing had happened. But one look at my face and she'd know.

I tiptoed up the steps to the door leading back into the parlor. I had heard someone confess to murder, and every nerve in me was stretched. I hated to leave Rita sitting there, but I needed to go home. Once I stepped inside, I made up my mind to walk straight through the parlor and out to the street.

Before I reached the top step, I saw from the corner of my eye the slight flutter of the blinds in the library. The open window overlooked the garden, and somehow I knew someone else had been watching.

Dad intercepted me the minute I stepped inside. "Where've you been? I wanted you to meet—"

I put my hands to my head. "Dad, not now. I—I don't feel too well . . ."

My eyes started to water and I blinked hard. Edwin Michaels's silky laughter rose from somewhere within a tight knot of men, and I felt a surge of bile rise to burn the back of my throat. I was so angry I was shaking.

"Dad, I've got to go . . . outside. Outside in the street for a minute."

If he had been annoyed, his irritation quickly gave way to concern. "Well, I . . . yes, okay."

I held my head down and allowed him to guide me to the door. In the foyer, a woman who had just arrived looked up from signing the guest book. She touched my arm. "You all right?"

I glanced at her, looked away, and then stared at her again—the woman with the feather cut who'd disappeared from Bert's the day after Thea died. Now she looked at me, concerned, and did not recognize me.

"I'm okay," I whispered.

On the way out, I managed to glance at the book.

Her name was Marian Prince and she lived somewhere on Hamilton Terrace.

Dr. Thomas had pulled more albums from his archives and Dad and I could hear Muddy Waters, Lionel Hampton, and Ella Fitzgerald from where we sat on our stoop two doors away. It was 1 A.M. and folks, well into CPT, were still arriving.

There was a breeze now, a faint one, that caused the shadows from the streetlight to shift as it filtered through the canopy of trees. I watched the shadows play against the gray pavement and remembered summer nights when I used to jump from shadow to shadow, trying to catch the light that I pretended were moonbeams. If I caught the beam, I believed I could float away to heaven.

I closed my eyes and opened them when Dad coughed.

"This is some deep, deep stuff, Mali. What you're tellin' me is damn deep."

I shrugged. Ordinarily, I would not have told him anything, I would not have involved him. But I remembered last summer when I'd gotten jammed and didn't tell him, he had been the one who had ended up in the hospital.

I watched him now as he shook his head.

"Who do you think was peeping through the blinds?"

"I don't know, Dad. Could've been anyone. I'll

just have to watch my back, wait until they play their hand."

I felt tired suddenly, and my anger boiled over at a dead woman who was still capable of destroying people from her grave.

Rita, I knew, would not be able to hold up much longer. There was too much pressure. Even if I hadn't eavesdropped, the way she handled those two martinis had said enough. And Edwin was not going to let her run around like a loose cannon.

"It's a matter of time, Dad. Something's going to happen to that girl."

He held up his hands. "Not necessarily. Whatever happens to her will have to happen to you also, and it will have to happen to me as well."

I turned to look at him and felt fear close in on me. Something was going to happen to my father?

"I figure it this way," he said. "Whoever peeped you back there had us in their sights when we walked out together. They probably think we're discussing it right now. So unless they're planning to wipe out—erase—a whole circle of folks, there's not much they can do except sit tight."

I leaned back gazing at him as he rested his head against the railing. *Sit tight.* A major elective office was at stake. What on earth did Thea have that would make a senator jeopardize his career? He had written to her, bared his soul on paper. Could a man really get that crazy?

Then again, what made a presidential adviser allow a two-hundred-dollar-an-hour prostitute to listen in on confidential White House phone calls and read documents even before the president had seen them?

Michaels wasn't crazy, but just another victim of Lettie's syndrome who was about to be exposed when the shit hit the fan.

I looked at Dad, wanting to believe that everything was going to be all right. But the thin scar was still faintly visible down the left side of his face, and I heard the slight rasp in his voice that made him cough every now and then, especially when he was nervous or upset.

These were the battle wounds from last summer, when a bunch of drug-dealing rogue cops had tried to get to me. They'd been brought down, but not before Dad had been badly hurt. After that, I had resolved to mind my own business.

I looked around me now and wondered what had happened, how I'd gotten drawn into this new thing. I'd been worried about how Alvin would react to Kendrick's being in jail. Alvin looked up to Kendrick. And I loved Kendrick like a brother. Flyin' Home may or may not have been killed because of my nosiness. And there was that white woman offering me money to poke around in black folks' business, then suddenly backing away.

And worst of all, when Tad comes home, I'd have to tell him how I'd gotten involved, even though he'd warned me not to. How did all this happen? Well, to hell with it. From now on, let Bert work this show herself. Get her own brother out. And to hell with Teddi and her stupid obsession. My father means too much. I would tell Bert tomorrow that friend or not, I'm out.

Dad rose from the stoop and stretched. With his arms out, he resembled an eagle ready to soar against the night sky. He lowered his arms slowly and beckoned.

"Come on."

"Where?"

"Back to the party. I want to tell Blaine I'm taking a rain check. The folks'll have to make do with his albums."

I stared at him, unable to move. I could not face Edwin Michaels and I could not let my father go back there without me.

"Couldn't you phone?"

"No. He'd never understand that. My name's on that invitation. I need to see him."

Which meant that Dad was going to tell him about Edwin, Thea, Rita, Henderson Laws, and the letter. He was going to tell everything. Blaine Thomas and my father went back a long way. You couldn't tell half a story to a forty-year friend. He'd guess the other half before the telling was over.

I rose to my feet, prepared to follow him even though my legs were shaking.

We had not taken two steps when the door opened and Blaine rushed out and sprinted to the door of a waiting Cadillac. Behind him, two men hurried out carrying a woman. Her feet did not touch the steps. They placed her in the backseat and Edwin Michaels followed, quickly closing himself behind the darkened windows.

People crowded the foyer, whispering as the car pulled away. At the corner its dome light and siren came on as it cut into the traffic of Eighth Avenue.

"What the hell happened?"

Blaine turned to face us, his expression one of blank surprise. "It's Anne. She's unconscious. They're taking her to the hospital. She opened the cabinet in the library and drank almost an entire bottle of Scotch. This woman never touched a drop of alcohol in her life. Can you imagine?"

I knew then that Anne had been the one in the window, and even if she hadn't heard every word clearly, she surely heard enough to confirm her worst suspicions. She had watched her husband smooth Rita's hair, touch her face, and kiss her.

Through her tears—there had to have been tears—Anne had watched him stroke a woman who had murdered for him.

chapter twenty-one

When Gladys called, I should have refused. I was not up to returning to Thea's apartment, but I had been so willing to help earlier that I couldn't back away now. And I was still struggling with what to do about Rita. For the last twenty-four hours, the three of us—Dr. Thomas, Dad, and I—had a running argument about what I'd overheard.

Dr. Thomas felt I should go to the police. I felt confused and wished I'd never heard of Rita Bayne, wished I'd never stepped into that garden.

I couldn't go to the police, not yet anyway. Suppose she hadn't really done it—just told Edwin that tale to keep him close. Suppose it had only been those martinis setting fire to her imagination. And suppose it had been someone other than Anne at that window. That person had seen me leave with Dad. I'd made up my mind to keep quiet, even if it meant having a sleazy politician win the election. Worse folks have been in office. Michaels was no different. I repeated this argument until I was dizzy, but still couldn't convince myself that I was doing the right thing. I also had not called Bert, and now here I was going back to the apartment of the woman who had started all of this.

When I arrived, Gladys was already upstairs in the living room, where two packing boxes lay open near the fireplace.

"A lot of this stuff will have to be stored until her estate is settled," she said.

"Did Thea leave a will?"

"Yes. And some interesting surprises as the dead are wont to do."

I took a seat on the ottoman and waited as she brought an armload of clothing from the larger bedroom.

"Surprises like what?" I asked.

"Like her income, for one thing. One thousand a month from her husband, one thousand a month from her boyfriend."

"Not bad," I said. "I suppose most of it went to furnish this place."

"Oh no. I went with her to set up an IRA, and another time to purchase certificates of deposit. I thought it was a one-time thing. I had no idea that her income was so . . . steady."

I didn't answer. Roger and Edwin gave her two thousand. Who was shelling out the rest? Laws? Or maybe it was Roger and Laws for certain and Edwin was the wild card. I shuffled the names around in my head. Edwin told Rita he was expecting some money soon. And one hundred thousand wasn't about to fall in his lap from a tree. I nearly smiled at the thought of him stealing his own money back—and someone else's as a bonus.

"Did Roger ever mention how much he was sending her?"

"No. I haven't spoken to him since the service. She mentioned it in her notebook."

"How come the police didn't find that book?"

"Thea had hidden it in a box of sanitary napkins."

"Did Roger or her boyfriend have a key to this place?"

"I'm not sure. Why?"

"Well, until you get everything cleared up, you might want to change these locks. When I was on the force, I saw whole apartments emptied out while the relatives were at the funeral. Truck backed up to the door and even took the food intended for the wake.

"I also saw a sister have her brother arrested for wiping out their mother's checking account while the woman's body was still at the undertaker's. Not even in the ground yet. People can do wonders with a computer and an ATM these days. All they need is a Social Security number. So if Thea had any accounts . . ."

"You're right. I've been so busy I didn't think of it."

I left her and wandered into the small bedroom. The chest and dresser drawers were open and empty, and I moved beyond them to stand near the bed.

"Who designed this?" I asked, running my hand

over the quilted headboard. Gladys had poured two drinks and followed me to the doorway, and extended a glass to me. I couldn't decide if alcohol was part of her daily diet or a temporary crutch to get through this period.

"A boyfriend," she said, "had that piece custom-made."

"It's unusual," I said, still running my hands over the surface. My fingers slid down the side and came to rest on the zipper. "What's this?"

"What's what?" Gladys stepped into the room and leaned over the bed. "Well, damn. I'll be damned."

I pulled the zipper back and expressed surprise. "It's empty."

"So it appears," Gladys said, more to herself than to me.

"I don't want to sound paranoid," I said, "but maybe that's where she kept her jewelry and—"

"Thea had very little jewelry. Said she never wanted to sell or pawn anything. She believed in cash and money in the bank where she could see the figures."

Gladys walked to the window, then moved slowly back to the living room, where she rummaged through her bag and pulled out her cell phone. She made two brief calls, then returned to the room and slipped her fingers into the empty space.

"Edwin had this bed made up for her. He knew what was in here." She turned to me, frowning. "Edwin's not smart; he's slick, but not too bright. And he's a pussy hound. That's what's going to bring him down eventually. I don't know how his wife puts up with it."

"Maybe she loves him too much to leave," I said.

"And look where it got her. In the hospital drifting in and out of a coma."

In the living room, Gladys continued to pack the boxes.

"Who do you think killed Thea?" she asked.

The question took me by surprise, and when I didn't answer she stopped packing, sat down on the sofa, and picked up her glass again. She studied the amber liquid and squinted as if the answer was floating somewhere under the ice cubes.

"You know what I think, Mali? I think she murdered herself."

"Really?" It was my turn to sit down now. "She didn't commit suicide."

"No, no. By that I meant she had absolutely no interest in living."

"Did Thea—did she talk often about how she felt about her life?"

"Well, that notebook you saw, and those letters . . . The notebook was filled with nothing but heartache. Page after page after page. She hated everybody, most of all herself."

"Why?"

"I don't know. The writing was so disjointed I couldn't get past the first few pages. It didn't seem like the Thea I knew, so I stopped reading."

"Where's the book now?"

Gladys rose from the sofa and walked to the foyer, then retraced her steps. The silence was broken by the small clicks of the ice cubes in her glass.

"Where's the book?" I asked again.

She stopped moving but did not look at me.

"Mali, I . . . wanted to preserve my memory of her. And my sanity. So I destroyed it, along with the letters."

I stared at her. I couldn't believe what I was hearing. "Memory! Sanity! Gladys, there may've been something in that book to prove Kendrick didn't kill her!"

"Well, I'm sorry. I'm sorry about that. What's done is done. I wanted to preserve her memory as is, Mali. You'll never understand. We were beautiful. We were queens, if only for a minute. And for her to die that way—in some filthy alley with half her face gone. That's not the Thea I want to remember."

"Even if an innocent man may have to spend perhaps the rest of his life in jail?"

She did not answer but placed her drink on the coffee table and resumed filling the boxes. I watched her work, and the urge to hit her was so strong I turned and walked to the bathroom to be out of her way. I looked in the cabinet at several jars of makeup and I opened each one. I thought of the dim lights in the club and the smoky scene at the Half-Moon. Makeup that was laid on heavy looked normal in those instances, but here was jar upon jar—some barely touched, others deeply gouged—of makeup shades radically different from her natural complexion. As if she had been searching for just the right mask.

I heard the doorbell ring, then Gladys called me from the living room, and I closed the jars. A locksmith had arrived. As he worked, I went from room to room for one last look around. When I left this time, I knew I wouldn't be back.

chapter twenty-two

On Saturday morning, three days after the party, Rita Bayne swallowed a fistful of diet pills and sleeping pills and washed them down with a half a fifth of vodka.

The news spread like a wave as people worked the connection between Michael's wife and his assistant—both hospitalized and both in critical condition.

Dad hung up the phone after speaking with Dr. Thomas. "We should've gone to the police. Blaine thinks it's a suicide attempt, but I think somebody's trying to shut her up."

I put down the coffee cup and squeezed my eyes shut. I had known something was going to happen. But not this way. An overdose. I wondered if Michaels was behind this, trying to clean up. And I wondered if Rita had given up the letter.

"She's in Harlem Hospital," Dad continued.

"Poor thing. Got into this mess way over her head, and then ends up like this. Michaels is gonna pay for it."

Indeed he will, I thought, but how? When?

Despite Wednesday night's promise—to mind my business, to lay off and let Bertha handle whatever was going to happen—I found myself dressing quickly, and fifteen minutes later I walked into the crowded lobby of the hospital.

The information clerk tapped the computer and read from the screen: "Critical condition, not receiving visitors."

"What room is she in? I'd like to send flowers."

"Room 401."

"Thank you," I murmured. I walked across the lobby to mingle with a small group heading toward the elevator.

"Miss?" The guard signaled and I smiled, pointing toward the group. I knew there were several conference rooms on the second floor, and I said, "I'm here for a meeting."

He waved me on and I managed to catch the elevator just as the door was closing.

I stepped off on the fourth floor. Marian Prince was walking toward me, and I watched her walk past the nurse's station in the center and glance up, distracted by the sound of activity. A second later, she moved on, gliding in the slow silence of a sleepwalker. I waited near the elevator until she pressed the button, and when it arrived I stepped inside with her.

"Miss Prince?"

She looked up as if I'd startled her out of a dream.

"Yes? Oh! You . . . were at that party. Your eyes . . . I recognize . . ."

The door opened on the third floor and a crowd pushed their way in, separating us. Marian leaned against the far wall and was silent until we stepped into the lobby.

"You were at that party," she said again, "and weren't feeling well when I saw you."

"Yes. I'm Mali Anderson. I'm sorry about Rita. I was just coming to visit her."

Marian nodded as if trying to shake herself out of a daze. "Yes. I arrived at that party very late. Did anything happen before I . . ." Her voice trailed off and I waited a second before I answered.

"I was talking to Rita near the buffet table and she seemed to have gotten a little upset about something. She disappeared, and the next thing I hear, she's in the hospital. How's she doing?"

"I don't know. I couldn't get in to see her. She's my sister and—"

"Your sister?"

"Yes. And there's a guard outside her room. He wouldn't let me near her. I mean it's not as if she has AIDS or that new TB or something. Why have they isolated her? I'm going to see the administrator about this. I—my sister is in critical condition and someone needs to tell me what's going on."

People moved around us toward the lobby doors, the elevators, the information booth. The neon above the entrance to a McDonald's flashed like a rainbow, but Marian seemed rooted to the spot, her eyes fixed in the distance.

"Come on," I whispered, "we'll have a cup of coffee."

"No. I can't leave here. Not until someone tells me what's going on."

"Maybe," I said, "the administration decided to bar all visitors considering the circumstances . . . you know—Anne Michaels's situation and now this. The media'll try to get to your sister. They're like vultures. They'll fly through the window to get to her no matter what shape she's in. And you have a different last name. You—"

"I married and divorced," she snapped. "I kept my married name, but I can certainly prove I'm a Bayne. And who are you? A cop or—"

"No. No ma'am. I'm just a friend who's concerned about what happened."

Her expression softened and she regarded me for a minute before she spoke again. "I'm sorry. You can see how upset I am about this. How well do you know Rita?"

The voice had not softened entirely and I decided to be only half-truthful. "I met her a few days ago in the Pink Fingernail. A friend of mine owns the place."

Marian nodded. "Oh yes, Vivian. She did a makeover."

"And I spoke to Rita quite awhile at the party. She seemed nervous but I thought it was because of the crowd, the event itself. You know: Some folks just don't like that sort of excitement.

"She had two martinis while we talked, but when Edwin Michaels walked in, she left me to go find the bathroom. I went looking for her, thinking she'd gotten sick. It was a while before I found her."

"Where was she?"

"Out in the garden."

"With Edwin?"

"Yes."

"Shit! I knew it!"

Marian looked away and I knew she wanted to ask me what I'd heard or seen.

"Come on," she said, heading for the door.

"Where?"

"Across the street. Singleton's restaurant. We can't talk in here."

The lunchtime crowd had not arrived yet so we had a choice of tables. We took one in the back, ordered the lunch special, and as soon as the waiter disappeared Marian held her head in both hands. "I . . . don't know where all this will end. Or how. From the start, that bastard took advantage of my sister. She's young, was only out of college a few years when she went to work for him. I saw it coming, but she was in a love fog and couldn't see two feet in front of her. Couldn't see the man's wife, or that bitch Thea.

"Sometimes I think Rita has cried more about Thea than about the fact that Edwin is married. And she sees how badly he treats his wife. Why does she think he would treat her any differently? She's in a real fog."

"Love will do that," I said, trying to keep my voice

even. I had no intention of telling what I'd overheard. Rita had killed a man and now she was hospitalized, probably hanging on by a thread. If she went, her secret would go with her, or at least I wouldn't be the one to tell it.

The waiter returned with two oversize plates of fried chicken wings, collard greens, and potato salad.

Grief usually suppressed the appetite, but Marian dug into her plate as if this were her first meal in a week.

"Were you at the Half-Moon that night?" I asked.

"When Thea was killed? Oh yes."

Between bites, she continued. "You see, I try to get to as many places where I know Rita'll be. I sort of drop in. Especially where there's bound to be alcohol, because when she's stressed she can't, as the old folks say, hold her liquor. That's why I was at Dr. Thomas's house. I'm not one of those political high rollers on someone's A-list. I showed up there because of my sister."

"Why does Edwin keep her on his staff?" I asked.

"Well, at first I wanted to believe it was because she was a good worker, but when I found out the real deal, I figured it was ego, mainly. He knew from the start that he affected her in certain ways, and I think he enjoyed watching her fall apart from time to time. Then he'd step in and build her up again, promise by promise."

"But meanwhile," I said, "he was falling apart over Thea."

"I suppose so. Perhaps that's why he needed my sister. As a counterbalance."

We ate in silence and I thought of the two women, one dead and one hospitalized, who couldn't have been more different, both entangled with the same man.

"Like I said," Marian continued, "I was in the bar that night. Place struck me as sleazy the minute I walked in, but Rita was there so I stayed."

"You saw Thea?"

"Oh yes. Very pretty. Stunning, you might say, but seemed as if she'd been carved from ice. I mean she sat there as if she was not really connected with anything that was going on in that place. When Edwin gave her an envelope, Rita saw it also, and I thought my poor sister was going to say something. But she was cool. She amazed me.

"When all hell broke loose following the shooting, Edwin disappeared. Probably jumped into the first thing rolling. We blinked and he was in the wind.

"In the confusion, we saw Henderson help himself to the envelope that was in Thea's purse. The police had come in by then and everybody had to leave. There was only Rita and me and maybe another woman inside. Everyone else was out in the alley. So much screaming and yelling . . . I didn't want to go out there."

"And you came to Bertha's the next day."

She stopped eating and stared at me, suspicion dawning again. "How did you know that?"

"I was there when you walked in with that other woman."

"What do you do? Hang out in hairdressers' as a hobby?" She stared at my hair as she said it and I had to smile. "Vivian and Bertha are friends of mine. I've known Bertha eighteen years. How'd you find her place?"

"How'd I find it? She was screaming and advertising loud enough to even wake up Thea. Yelling that she was a beautician who paid her taxes and the police had better not lay a hand on her brother. As soon as she said the name, I knew where her shop was. Bertha's Beauty Shop, right there on Eighth Avenue."

"Do you think her brother did it? Killed Thea?" I asked.

She lifted her shoulders. "I don't know. He was crying and I heard him, as clear as if he'd been standing next to me, saying he didn't mean it. He didn't mean it. Now what was that all about? And where's the weapon? Maybe he did it and someone else picked up the gun. There're too many unanswered questions, so I really don't know."

We were silent as people entered and stood at the take-out window at the front of the restaurant. Marian continued to eat.

"Kendrick's like a brother to me," I said, breaking the silence. "He helped me when I was going through a bad time after my sister died. He was there for my nephew, and now I'm trying to help him. My nephew'll be back from vacation soon and I promised myself that Kendrick'd be out of jail before then. Now, I don't know how I could've made such a promise . . ."

She dipped her fork in the greens and I marveled that she was able to eat at all. A minute later, she put down her fork and passed her hand over her face.

"Anything wrong?" I asked.

"Aren't you a police officer?" she whispered, staring at me intently.

"I was, very briefly, a few years ago."

"I thought I recognized you. You undercover or you really quit?"

"I was fired for hitting another cop," I said. "He couldn't keep his dirty mouth shut so I shut it for him. I'm suing for wrongful dismissal."

"Well, I'll be damned." She whistled softly and looked at me with dawning admiration. "Who's your attorney? I'm going to need one if they decide to play games with me." She gestured across the street. "If I can't get to see . . ."

"Elizabeth Jackson," I said, writing her name and phone number on a napkin. "She's also handling Kendrick's case. High-powered sister."

She put the folded napkin into her shoulder bag and brought out an envelope. She slid it across the table, where it rested against the saltshaker. "I can see you didn't particularly like Thea, or Edwin either, for that matter. Take this. Read it when you get home."

The lunchtime crowd had moved in now and conversation in the low octaves was impossible. I passed up the sweet-potato pie, paid the check, and we left.

Outside, Marian gazed across the avenue at the entrance to the hospital. I waited, watching the whirl of activity on the avenue: folks rushing from the subway, swirling around a cadaverous crackhead holding a dingy paper cup; lines of vendors moving fast, pushing shopping carts filled with flowers, fruits, cakes and pies, and coconut-flavored ices.

In front of the hospital, women with baby strollers sunned themselves on the stone ledges. A block away, near the parking lot, an old man tipped his chair back against the fender of his watermelon truck, sound asleep despite the noise of traffic and nearby construction.

Finally, Marian said, "I'm going to see my sister. I'll call your attorney if they keep me out."

"You want me to go with you?"

"No. No, I can handle this myself."

"All right." I rummaged in my bag for my card. "Call me and let me know if you need anything else. Or if you just feel like talking."

"If I feel like—listen . . ." She put her hand to the side of her face, holding it as if it hurt.

"Mali, do you know what Edwin's like? I mean behind those thousand-dollar suits and that million-dollar smile? You have no idea, have you?"

"I know I don't like him. Never have. Never will."

"Well, I'm telling you this: If Rita doesn't pull through . . ."

She stopped and looked away. "Last year, Edwin arranged to take her to St. Thomas. She was ecstatic, poor thing. Couldn't stop talking about it. When they arrived at the hotel, who do you think she found there?"

"Thea?"

Marian nodded, her eyes bright with anger. "Edwin had booked them in separate rooms and took turns. When Rita found out, she came home. I met her at the airport and her eyes were nearly swollen shut from cry-

ing. You have no idea how I despise that man. If anything happens, the media will hear from me and a
whole lot of other people . . ."

Without another word, she walked off and crossed
against the traffic, and I watched her disappear through
the entrance of the hospital. I walked away, and turned
at 136th Street, walking past the Countee Cullen Library, where a group of day-campers were filing in for
story hour. At Seventh Avenue and 137th Street, I
couldn't wait to get home so I reached into my bag and
tore open the envelope.

Dearest Thea,

    You are determined to have this baby. As I told
you last week, the timing couldn't be worse. October is a crucial month, especially in the voters'
minds. You'll be six months by then. But I think I
understand why you want this child. I've arranged
for you to spend the final three months in St.
Thomas. The condo is private and you won't have
to lift a finger except to call me and let me know
what you need. You know how I feel. This is my
child too so I'll take care of everything. You are
what I want and what I've always wanted. I would
kill to keep you. I hope you will understand and
not make things too unpleasant for us. You know I
love you.

Edwin

P.S. My investigator came across an old New York
Times photo. An interesting one. Perhaps you'd

like to see it? Anyway, let me know what you decide. I love you despite everything and more than anything.

I sat down on the concrete ledge of the traffic island and gazed at the rush of cars. Across the street, a small crowd had gathered outside the Rodney Dade Funeral Home. The mourners were young with caps turned back and grief shaded behind small round sunglasses. A young woman in a long cotton skirt and matching head wrap pushing a cart of groceries paused near me and also watched. "Child wasn't more than fourteen," she said. "They're leaving here younger and younger, and the rest just don't seem to get the message."

I thought of Rita, also young but too much in love to listen to the advice of an older sister, and now Marian was rushing to get to her bedside.

chapter twenty-three

I think he did it," Bertha said, leaning back in her chair and staring out the window at the early-Saturday-evening traffic. Bertha had just finished with one customer and the six-o'clock appointment had not yet shown up. We were alone in the shop and Bert had turned down the television's volume. Even though I had a problem with those mind-numbing soap operas, game shows, and tell-all talk shows, I realized now in the thick silence how much they meant to her.

She had turned off the sound and the chaos of make-believe lives in order to grab at this latest straw, and I was embarrassed that I'd earlier thought of abandoning her.

"Yep. I think Edwin Michaels is the one. He killed Thea."

"But he was still in the bar when it happened," I reminded her. "You said you saw him."

"Well, then. He coulda paid somebody to cap her.

That don't take much. Get the right crackhead, they'd do it for food stamps."

I pointed to the letter in her hand, showing her the postscript. "If he had planned to kill her—or have her killed—do you think he would've bothered with this letter? Not likely."

"Well, then, maybe it was that fool Rita. From what you told me, she sure had enough reason to want Thea out the way."

I nodded and was quiet for a moment. I had no intention of revealing that Rita had killed Henderson Laws. That night, while Rita'd been in confessional mode, she would've mentioned killing Thea too. She'd had enough alcohol on her brain to confess to a lot of things, and one more body wouldn't have made a difference.

"If you look close enough," I said, "you might see that Anne Michaels also had good reason to kill Thea. Don't think she didn't know what her husband was up to."

"Well," Bert said, "we got a truckload of maybes, but it was Laws who ran out there and pinned it on Kendrick."

I poured another cup of coffee and returned to sit on the chair opposite her.

And it occurred to me that Kendrick had been denied bail not because of some remote possibility of skipping the country, but because someone—with authority—had called the judge for a favor. Laws put him in jail, but Michaels and a crooked political system had most likely kept him there.

"Kendrick's in protective custody," Bert said as if she'd read my thoughts. "At least he ain't fightin' so much anymore. I thought for sure he was gonna get his face marked up before he gets outta there."

She rose and began to pace the floor from the door to her chair and back again. "Tell me something: If that white woman is so much in love, and her money's so damn long, why ain't she buyin' a judge to spring him? She got the power."

"She may have the power, but what if she no longer has the will? As you said, suppose Kendrick told her he wasn't interested, do you think she'd still—"

The bell jingled softly. I looked up to see Tad standing in the open door.

"Hi. Do I need an appointment or do you accommodate walk-ins?" He stepped inside and leaned against the closed door, smiling a smile that looked almost radiant against his darkened skin. I sat there, staring.

Not only had my dream come true, but it had come looking for me. Damn!

I stared at him and imagined myself rising from the chair, forgetting all about Bertha, and floating slow-motion, like in that classic scene in *Sounder* when Cicely Tyson's husband returns from wherever he'd been for the last ten years.

I was in fact on my feet, moving, when Bertha broke the spell: "Well, hello! Who sent this fine package? If it's from UPS, I hope they *never* go on strike."

Tad's skin had darkened too much to betray a

significant blush, but he looked at me, glanced down at
the floor, and then smiled.

"I stopped by your place. Wanted to surprise you.
Your Dad said you might be here, at your cool-out spot.
So: How've you been?"

He was being polite and formal, but that low-bass
whisper was like a heat-seeking missile, and right on
target.

"Fine," I said, then kissed him a small kiss but
wanting to taste all of his tongue and tonsils too. "Fine."

Bertha watched from her chair, beaming, and
seemed to light up even brighter when he turned to her.
"How're you doing, Bertha?"

"Fine. Just fine. Not bad at all."

"Good. What's happening with your brother?"

Her smile disappeared, and she remembered that
she wasn't doing so fine.

"He's still down at detention."

And my smile faded also as she continued. "But
your girl here is doin' the best she can to help get him
cleared. She's right in the middle of things. As a matter
of fact, we were just tryin' to figure . . ." I listened to
her go on and on until finally she said, "She's almost as
good a detective as you are. You oughtta be proud of
her."

I had been standing next to Tad. His hand was on
my shoulder and I felt the pressure of his fingers stead-
ily increasing as Bertha spoke.

"Well, really, Bert," I murmured, "I didn't do
much at all."

Tad shifted from one foot to the other and said, "Mm-hmm. She's quite a girl."

"You tellin' me? Couldn't ask for better. She's like the sister me and my brother never had."

She looked up and smiled at me and I wanted to cry.

Tad looked at me and I shrugged—or tried to. "It wasn't all that," I said lamely.

The bell jingled again and a young woman came in pushing a stroller. Tad held the door open and helped her maneuver the carriage inside. The baby boy, about six months old, was asleep.

"I had to wait," she said, "till he decided to take a nap. I'm sorry I'm late."

I'm sorry also, I thought as Tad moved toward the door, guiding me firmly in front of him.

Eighth Avenue on Saturday evening was usually pretty lively, and Alvin and I loved to walk with Ruffin for blocks and blocks. Folks sat in front of houses, or under the streetlights crowded around small card tables where the slap of cards and dominoes rose above the small talk. Knots of teenagers lounged on benches near the projects eating fish 'n' chips and snapping to rap. The smaller kids, when they saw Alvin leading the big Great Dane, rushed over to us, wanting to pet Ruffin as though he were a toy horse. "Aw, Miss Mali, just one time . . . ," even though I had to say no every time.

The hum of activity was there as Tad and I

strolled up Eighth Avenue, and past the new Strivers Row town houses. But between us was a deep vacuum in which not one word was spoken since we'd left Bertha's.

Though we'd had no reservations at Londel's, Tad knew the manager and we were able to get a table outdoors. Once we were seated, and dinner and drinks ordered, he looked at me.

"Okay: Care to tell me what's been happening while I was away?" His voice was even and his eyes were pools of smoke.

I stared back and did not waver as I began to speak, recounting the events from the time Bertha had called crying on the phone near the Half-Moon. I spoke about TooHot and what he'd said about Laws and Kendrick. I mentioned how Flyin' Home had seen someone leave the alley and how I had wanted him to talk to the police but he'd gotten killed. I spoke of Teddi Lovette, who was in love with Kendrick, and my meeting her and her bigoted mother at the theater.

Dinner was placed on the table but Tad pushed his plate aside and continued to write in the small notepad he'd taken from his vest pocket.

"And you say Thea was married to Roger Morris? Morris, the architect?"

"Yes."

And finally, reluctantly, I spoke of Rita's confession to Edwin Michaels, and how she'd described killing Henderson Laws. I did not want to do that, but if this puzzle was going to be put together, all the pieces, no matter how painful, had to be laid on the table.

He closed the notepad and looked at me for several seconds.

"You know," he whispered, taking my hands in his, "aside from the fact that I love the hell out of you, you're quite a girl, Mali. You're damn special. You zero in and don't give up. I wish the hell you were back on the force."

"Never mind the force," I whispered, feeling the warmth of his fingers. "Did you miss me?"

"Did I miss—? Ah, Baby, come here . . ."

He leaned over, held my face in his hands, and kissed me hard enough to make my teeth hurt. When he let me go and rested his elbows on the table, he knocked over his water glass. Diners nearby smiled and one guy actually lifted his own glass. "Bless you, brother. If I had me a fine honey like that, I'd be a little crazy myself."

The brother making the toast was feeling no pain, and Tad nodded and turned to gaze at me again.

"Are you really hungry?"

"For what?" I whispered.

"Dinner."

"Depends on the menu," I said, running my fingertips lightly against his open palm.

"How about dessert? Dark chocolate filled with whipped cream?"

"That's fattening," I said.

"Yeah, but we can work it off, baby."

He paid the bill and the waiter eyed the untouched plates. "Something wrong with the food, sir?"

"No, my man, not at all. But something important just came up."

chapter twenty-four

t three o'clock on Monday afternoon, Rita Bayne died of respiratory failure.

On Tuesday, true to her word, Marian Prince delivered to the media copies of her sister's handwritten confession, copies of Edwin's letter to Thea, and the canceled checks he'd given her over the years. Thea had been paid from Michaels's office accounts, and Rita had handled all the finances.

Marian also delivered the copies to Dora Peterson's campaign people.

The senator called a press conference. I wasted a few seconds trying to adjust the television when he came on the six-o'clock news but then realized that the ashen tinge on his brown skin was not likely to go away.

He was surrounded by grim-looking campaign aides, a minister, and a tearful young woman who may have been his daughter. Dad and I listened as he read his statement:

"I am terminating my campaign for reelection and resigning my office in order to devote more time to my wife and family. As you know, my wife is currently hospitalized in critical condition due to an unfortunate accident. I need to be at her side through the coming weeks and with your prayers help her pull through this difficult period. Thank you."

He did not look up from the paper in his hand, he did not mention Rita Bayne's death, and he did not answer questions about his letter, his payments to the murdered Thea Morris, or his connection to Henderson Laws, also found murdered.

Dad clicked the remote and the screen went dark. "Media's gonna give him hell."

"He deserves it," I said, amazed at the gall of a politician when he's caught with his pants down. It was standard practice to trot out the old "wife and family" alibi, the need to be with them in a time of crisis.

"How come," I asked Dad, "Michaels didn't think about his wife when he was carrying on like a dog and chasing every leg that passed his way? Now Rita's gone. All because of a dumb letter written by a stupid man to a woman who never really gave a damn about any-one . . ."

Dad looked at me. "You're getting worked up, Mali. Michaels is out. Rita is gone. She's gone. You can't bring her back. You gotta let it lay. Ain't but so much juice you can suck from a dry bone."

"Let it lay? Kendrick's still in jail. How can I let it lay?"

He didn't answer and clicked the remote again,

surfing the channels. There was Marian Prince on New York 1, in front of the wrought-iron gates of her sister's apartment building surrounded by newspeople.

"Senator Michaels caused my sister's death as surely as if he'd held a gun to her head. He's responsible for her death, and probably for Thea Morris's death, and even for Henderson Laws's death. The police need to look at all of that because surely there's a connection."

Her sunglasses hid her grief and her voice was soft but she spoke directly into the camera as she held up the letters.

"He abused my sister and the trust my family had in him. He may be out of office but I won't rest until he pays for what he's done to my sister."

I didn't want to see any more and left the room. Too many questions were moving around in my head. And all led back to square one. Who had killed Thea?

chapter twenty-five

The sound of the door closing woke me and I climbed out of bed in time to see Dad stroll down the block with Ruffin, heading toward St. Nicholas Park. Long after they disappeared in the morning fog, I remained at the window, gazing out at the wet pavement. Rain had come sometime during the night and had tapered off just before dawn, leaving a mist the sun would later burn off.

Standing there, I felt as if something cold had passed through the window to settle in my bones, making me forget that it was an August morning.

I pressed my face to the window, thinking of Rita Michaels's announcement had sent a jolt through the community, and today's papers would probably be saturated with analyses and innuendo. But behind it all, Kendrick, the forgotten man, was still in jail.

"We can get him out, Bert. We can get him out. . . ." I had said it and not known how I was going

to do it. At one point, I'd even wanted to give up and let Bertha go solo. The idea embarrassed me now.

I thought of Gladys again, savoring four fingers of Scotch on the rocks, and determined in her way to preserve a memory of a ghost no one had known.

"What's done is done. I wanted to preserve her memory as is, Mali. You'll never understand. We were beautiful. We were queens, if only for a minute. And for her to die that way—in some filthy alley with half her face gone. That's not the Thea I want to remember."

I thought of Teddi Lovette, with her nervous fingers moving through her hair, moving along the edge of Thea's casket, maneuvering around the brittle relationship with her mother. And her love for a man whose blackness her mother probably hated and would've donated her last dollar to keep him behind bars and away from her daughter.

I wondered what Teddi'd make of the latest news.

I wondered about Elizabeth and what strategy she intended to use now. The way things appeared, the prosecutor could make a case that Kendrick killed Thea because he was jealous of her involvement with Michaels.

Flyin' Home was gone. Thea's diary was gone. Rita was gone. Whatever information anyone had was lost. What's done is done . . .

I turned my head against the voice, and the cold of the window pierced the side of my face like a toothache. The I heard something—or someone else—somewhere in the still room. I did not look around this time either for my mother's presence because I knew I wouldn't find her.

"There's more than one way to skin a cat. I keep telling you that. Don't you remember anything I say?" A mantra to strengthen the mind-set. A statement of purpose. Her prelude to probing whatever it was that cried out for a solution.

. . . *Skin a cat.* I had heard this when I was young enough to still lose myself in the literal landscape of my imagination and wonder why anyone would want to skin a cat in the first place.

I remembered my mother looking toward the ceiling, as if the strength to cope with my mental deficiency resided there.

"Just keep your mouth closed, your eyes open, and watch how it's done," she had said.

I had watched and learned a lot, but I needed her here now to show me once more how she did it.

The clock on the night table now read 9 A.M. and I sat on the edge of the bed and dialed a number, wondering if it was too early to be calling anyone.

Miss Adele picked up before the ring was completed, as if she had been waiting for me. Gospel music, strong and compelling, filled the background, but her voice rose above it.

"Did you have anything to do with this?" she asked by way of greeting. She was wide-awake and her deliberate tone barely hid the indignation simmering in the back of her throat.

"Anything to do with what?" I asked.

"With this . . . this damned story, this piece of trash in the paper."

"Which paper?" I knew Marian had contacted every media outlet she could think of, but why was Miss Adele asking me?

"Which paper?" I asked again.

"The damned so-called paper whose mission is to trash and demonize anyone and anything black, that's which paper!"

"No. No. Absolutely not. I—"

"Well, have you seen it? It's not about Michaels's resignation. It's an exposé of what had gone on at the Half-Moon. Thea's name and her pageant picture are splashed all over the front page. They're writing that she's responsible for Laws getting killed, for Anne's suicide attempt, and for that other girl killing herself. And they threw in some other stupid shit about Laws not cleaning the four corners of the bar. What the hell is that all about? And who cares? And as far as Thea is concerned, whoever threw the story together got the damn facts backward as usual, the son of a bitch."

I was amazed at the language. This classically trained Juilliard graduate who had enjoyed all those curtain calls at the Met was talking stuff strong enough to drain my earwax. I remained quiet and listened to the background rhythm of gospel as she applied more choice phrases to describe the newspaper. From time to time I nodded, not having bought that paper in years. I had given up trying to decode their creative grammar and misinformation some time ago. Nowadays I didn't even glance at the headlines for fear of being led astray.

"Miss Adele," I said as soon as I found a break, "I would not have spoken to any newsperson, especially one from downtown. My concern was to try to solve Thea's murder in order to get Kendrick out of jail. The little you told me, I've kept to myself. I haven't even discussed her with my dad, and you know she sang with the band.

"After I spoke to you, I managed to get that bankbook back where it belonged. While I was in the apartment, someone came in—a man. I hid under the bed. He took the bankbook. But he doubled back and caught me hiding, and I could've been killed but I never mentioned that to anyone. Not even to my dad."

"What? Who was it?"

"Probably Michaels. The room was dark, but even so I didn't hang around to check him out. But whoever it was is out of luck. I spoke to Gladys, and she's probably put a block on Thea's accounts by now."

"You thought to do all that?"

"Well, yes."

I could hear her breath coming slower now. We both listened to a full minute of gospel. Finally she said, "Girl, I knew your mama and daddy had raised you right. You are a wonder."

"Miss Adele, there's something I—"

She cut me off. "I want you to drop by for breakfast in an hour, you hear me?" And she hung up without a good-bye.

•   •   •   •

I sat in the dining alcove and Miss Adele apologized for the AC being off. "I can't stand all that humming when I'm trying to think."

She still walked barefoot and brought plates of French toast, bacon, and sausage to the table. When she popped a bottle of champagne without ceremony, I stared at the label.

"Dom Perignon? For breakfast?"

"My dear, I'm seventy-two years old. The only way to live long is to live well."

I watched her fill two crystal flutes and thought how Dad only popped this kind of grape once every five years on New Year's Eve. She extended a glass and drank before I could offer a toast.

I had no idea that champagne could turn an ordinary breakfast into a banquet, but it worked for me.

Miss Adele refilled the glasses and settled back. "I'm sorry to have to go through the long sad tale of Thea's life," she said. "We all *have* a sad story, but the trick is not to *become* a sad story.

"I know that young man is in jail for something he probably didn't do. I don't know who killed Thea, but I wasn't entirely truthful when you were here before."

I leaned back, imagining my mother nodding from a distance as Miss Adele continued.

"I mentioned how Dessie Hamilton had kept herself together after her world had blown apart, and even after her daughter Marcella had disappeared, leaving her to raise Thea.

"Well, when Dessie had gotten sick, Thea had

come home from the pageant. Dessie was in the hospital by then, and Thea was alone in the apartment. Went through Dessie's things looking for Medicaid papers or something, and came across Marcella's picture. She asked me who the woman was and I lied, said it was a friend of Dessie's. I figured Thea was upset enough and I didn't want things to get any worse. She had a good chance of winning that pageant, and I figured if she did, it would open up a new world for her and she wouldn't have time to think about the old one.

"I had to talk hard to get her back upstate for the finals. I told her I'd take care of everything. I'd take care of Dessie. But Thea must have known her grandmother wasn't going to make it.

"A few days later, Dessie died. Her liver just couldn't take the pressure of lifting a glass night after night every time someone offered a toast. I mean she enjoyed being a barmaid. She was attractive and the center of attention and all that excitement.

"You see, in those days the Half-Moon was the spot. I know because I dropped in every so often to see the musicians and the actors who wanted to be gangsters, and all those gangsters who wanted to be stars. Plus there were the regular politicians, and the big pimps dressed to the nines with their flashy women, and all the gamblers taking a break from their night jobs, just hanging out.

"Everybody knew Seventh Avenue was the strip with Small's Paradise, Count Basie's, Connie's Inn, Mr. B's Nightspot, Sugar Ray's, Shalimar, Jock's Place, and the Red Rooster. I could name all those flashing lights, but the Moon? There was no other place like it.

"I never stayed long because the smoke was bad for my throat and I had to protect my career. One drink and five minutes later, as much as I wanted to stay, I was out of there.

"But as I said, Dessie was in her element, and the older she got, the more glamorous she became. You wouldn't believe the serious proposals she turned down. Anyway, when she died I went to her place before Thea returned, and I got hold of that picture and the news clipping—"

"What clipping?"

"The wedding announcement in the *Times*."

"Who got married?"

"Thea's mama. Marcella."

"That made the *Times*?"

"Here, let me show you." She left the dining table and returned with a flat rosewood box inlaid with silver strips. She lifted the lid and handed me a photocopy of a barely legible article. The couple's features were indistinct and the writing was blurred either by age, water, or my having drunk too much so early in the day.

"That's Thea's mother. She changed her name, but it's the same person. Dessie knew Marcella was still alive; hadn't really died in California. She saw that announcement and kept track of her for years without telling Thea. Marcella married a very wealthy man and Dessie had made up her mind to let sleeping dogs lie. She figured she had done all right by Thea. No point in stirring up old dust."

"So you knew all along?" I asked.

Miss Adele refilled the glasses halfway and added a mix of orange and pineapple juices.

"Mali, when someone disappears—or abandons you—you hold out a hope that somehow, someday they'll come back into your life like magic and you'll live happily ever after.

"Dessie had had her share of fairy tales and no longer believed. But she knew death was permanent. Once a person crossed to the other side, they didn't come back, except in a dream to maybe give you a number. So she told Thea that her mother had died, killed in some car accident out West."

"How did Thea find out otherwise?"

"Dessie had an old hatbox that I didn't look in because I was so busy trying to clean out all the other stuff. I thought there were only hats in it. Instead it contained the news article and several letters she had written to Marcella but had never mailed. Thea found them and confronted me. I couldn't deny it. I told her everything, at least all that I knew. She walked out and that was the last time I saw her."

"How long ago was that?"

"I don't know. Five or six years ago. I blocked it out."

I leaned over the table and tried to study the picture again, but at this point my vision was so bad I knew I'd have to call a cab in order to get home. How could one bottle hold so many servings, I wondered as I held up my glass for yet another refill. My third and it was not yet noon.

We sat there sipping. Miss Adele seemed to cast off the years and we became contemporaries as talk detoured from one thing to another. When she laughed, her head tipped to the side and she opened her mouth wide, as if she were singing. When she spoke of Dessie, the sound grew deeper, richer.

"Do you know how many proposals—I mean *serious* proposals—that woman had by the time she was sixty?"

"How many?" I was fascinated, considering I'd had only four in my life and the only one I'd taken seriously was Ronald's—shy and handsome but already full of potential when he'd passed that note in the third grade asking to marry me when we grew up. I wondered what had become of him and if he'd ever stopped sucking his thumb.

"One dozen," Miss Adele said. "Can you imagine twelve offers of marriage and I myself only got to bury three husbands?"

"I can't imagine," I said, trying to hold on to the image of Tad, whose features were fast dissolving under the weight of the bubbly. That night at Londel's had been wonderful, and afterward at his place I had really welcomed him back home.

Miss Adele went to the fridge and brought out another bottle and I wondered who was going to drink all this stuff as I held up my glass for yet another round.

"You ever hear Thea sing?" she asked, changing the subject again.

"At the club," I said, hoping she wouldn't spoil the mood by asking what I thought of her performance.

"What did you think of her performance?" Miss Adele asked.

My wine-soaked conscience was a beat behind my tongue and I answered truthfully. "Not much. I mean, she didn't reach me. All I really remembered is her hand sweeping her hair from her face. I thought it was part of the act. I don't remember her voice at all."

Miss Adele shook her head, remembering also. "That was a nervous reaction. Something she did all her life."

I raised my glass to my mouth, hoping to end this part of the discussion and return to Dessie.

Dad had called her the world's oldest living barmaid, but according to Dessie age was just a number and the girl had it goin' on till the day she closed her eyes. She'd even walked to the hospital in five-inch heels. I liked her style.

"Dad said it takes quite a few years for a singer to develop," I added, trying to soften my hard opinion of Thea. I didn't want to offend Miss Adele, who, after all, had trained her.

"In fact, there's really no set time," she answered, glad to talk. "Some folks you have to nurse and bring along gradually. Others seem to burst on the scene like a meteor. Of course, they need direction also, to keep from burning out too quickly. But whether a singer develops over the years or overnight, she must have something to begin with. When I started to coach Thea, I knew she had something.

"You know how Nina Simone and Aretha Franklin can make you cry with a single note. You sit there in the dark listening and the tears are coming while you nod your head at something you wished you could've forgotten years ago. And then the very next song will have you smiling, stepping, finger-popping.

"Or go back earlier and listen to Billie Holiday sing 'Them There Eyes' or 'My Man.' That girl made you *see* what she saw, which was usually some pretty man whose mission was to dog you from day one. But you were able to *see* him and feel her pain, and that was her genius.

"Thea could've eventually done that, but for some reason . . ." Miss Adele sighed and the smile went away. "I can tell you why she lost that pageant, Mali. When she sang the crucial number, she was supposed to sing from her center—as most singers do. But Dessie, the only person in the world who had meant anything to her, was dying. And Thea's center drained like a whirlpool even as she fought to keep it intact.

"Then, a few years later when she found those letters, I imagine she really hollowed herself out. Emptied herself of everything. I mean what little that might have remained, she *froze* it, so to speak, then dug it out the way a dentist would handle a bad tooth. Then she filled that place with something that finally did her in."

"What was that?"

"Rage. Despair. Hopelessness. The knowledge that her mother had never wanted her and she had no idea who her father was. I don't think Dessie ever found out who Thea's father was. Marcella never said anything, only stayed one day and didn't even wave when she left. I know. And Thea must've found all that in those letters.

"She tried to sing after that, had several gigs here and there, but eventually she seemed to shut down, as if the world and everything in it was just too much."

"Is that why she went to work at the Half-Moon when she knew she could've done so much better? I mean, she had a modeling career, had married a successful architect. Why'd she throw that away?"

Miss Adele raised her shoulders gently, as if to shift a weight that had rested there too long.

"I don't really know. Perhaps she'd felt betrayed, violated. She'd lost a sense of who she was, and probably felt she didn't deserve anything that good. Who knows? Then again, she may have gone to the Half-Moon out of spite. By the time she started working there, the place was nothing like it used to be. It had gone through so many changes it gave me a headache just to pass by on the same side of the street."

"Maybe," I said, "it was her way of letting the world—especially her mother—know that she didn't care about anything. Nothing mattered."

Miss Adele nodded wearily. "For somebody who didn't care, she was a very busy girl."

I smiled, thinking of Edwin and all the other men in her life who had hoped to be the one to change her, to break through, like in *Pygmalion*. Instead, she had changed them. Or shortchanged them.

"Do you know of a woman named Teddi Lovette?" I asked, changing the subject again.

Miss Adele thought a minute, then shook her head. "Doesn't sound familiar. Who is she?"

"A white actress who has a small repertory company called Star Manhattan on Theater Row. She had asked me to find out as much as I could about Thea."

"Why?"

"She never gave me a clear answer. Except that she's in love with Kendrick and is kicking out big bucks for his legal fees."

"That's interesting. Seems to me she'd be concentrating on springing the living, not raising the dead. I mean, despite her money, Kendrick's still behind bars and—"

"She had offered me twenty thousand to dig up Thea . . . a hell of a lot of money. At first I thought it was because she was obsessed with the fact that Kendrick had been in love with Thea and she wanted to find out as much as possible about her. You know, find out the formula . . . But no damn formula is worth that much, even if Kendrick's a sixty-minute man. Then she changed her mind and told me to forget all about it."

Miss Adele put her glass down. "There must be something she isn't telling you, Mali. Listen: Give me her name again. Friend of mine was an assistant set designer when I was working. He's retired now but does some volunteer stuff in the small productions, especially along Theater Row, to keep his hand in. Something of a gossip, and he'll let me know what's going on in a beat."

• • •

I had no clear memory of arriving home. Just a wavery image of a cab waiting in front of Miss Adele's to pick me up, then a kaleidoscopic vision of trees, cars, horns, people, and Technicolor traffic lights. The sky was a painfully bright blue that wouldn't stop spinning whenever I looked up.

I did not remember how unsteady my hand was when I pushed a bill toward the driver, and I did not remember counting the change. Then came the careful and calculated tightwire stroll from the curb to the stoop and the relief that Dad had been waiting to open the door before the pavement, shimmering like waves, came up to meet my face.

He shepherded me inside and I heard succinct remarks but couldn't process them. Then more steps that he helped me negotiate and finally a cold cloth across my forehead. Before I drifted off, I saw golden starbursts explode like a Fourth of July gala, except all that terrific sound was entirely inside, ripping through my gray matter. The room was spinning and I thought, Miss Adele, Miss Adele. Living well is hell.

chapter twenty-six

There was a cup of coffee on the night table and it was dark outside when I turned over. The phone was ringing and I lay with eyes closed, preferring to let the machine click on. The message was faint—Dad must've turned the volume down low—and I didn't care so long as it didn't deepen the rhythm of the hammer in my head. I raised up on one elbow and leaned over to taste the coffee. It was ice-cold and I wondered vaguely how many hours had passed. The phone rang again and I ignored that call also. Then I fell back to sleep and somewhere between dreams I thought I heard it ring once more.

"You must have had quite a time at Adele's," Dad said as he pulled up the blinds. I blinked awake to the sun spilling yellow and white across my bed.

"What time is it?"

"You mean what day is it, don't you?"

I didn't answer and he closed the door, leaving me alone again. Actually I felt fine, having slept through the worst of the hangover. I showered quickly and wandered downstairs.

"Sorry, Dad. I hope I didn't embarrass you too much."

He looked up from the *Daily Challenge* and nodded. "Nope. You didn't embarrass me."

Which meant that I must have embarrassed myself. "It was champagne. Too much, too quick, too rich. Never again."

He didn't look up but riffled the papers in a way that let me know the subject was closed. I saw the tight expression and made up my own mind that popping corks was not for me.

Upstairs again, I turned on the answering machine and listened to two messages from Miss Adele asking me to call as soon as possible, and one from Teddi Lovette apologizing for her disappearing act the other day and promising to call later.

The phone rang again even as the last message played out.

"Mali," Miss Adele said without asking how I had survived her champagne breakfast. "I called my friend yesterday and he didn't even have to ask around. Your actress friend's maiden name is Teddi Eden. She's the daughter of Marissa and Sam Eden. Marissa Eden's maiden name is Hamil."

There was a pause and I waited. When Miss Adele didn't speak, I said, "Yes. Go on."

She laughed then. "You don't see?"

"See what?"

"The connection. The article I showed you yesterday."

"Oh. Oh," I said, even though I hadn't been able to make head or tails of the piece of paper. "Are you sure? I mean, is your friend sure?"

"Sure, he's sure. He knew Teddi's husband. Older man named William Lovette who died on the honeymoon. Left her megabucks and an estate in Westchester."

"Yes. Yes. But let's get back to Marissa Hamil. Or Eden. Or whatever her name is."

"Well, she was Marcella Hamilton before she was anything else," Miss Adele said. "Names may change but pictures don't lie."

I hung up and got out my file to jot down the latest developments. As I read it over, I didn't know whether to laugh or cry.

Later, I dialed Teddi's number, even though she'd told me not to. She was somewhere in Westchester, probably Bedford or Armonk, and I wondered about the size of her mansion. Her machine clicked and her voice sounded nervous even on the tape.

"Teddi, I have the information you wanted," I said and hung up without leaving my name. She'd know who I was.

It was 10 P.M. and I was wide-awake so I collared Ruffin. "Come on. Let's see what's happening at Better Crust Pie Shop. I need a sweet-potato custard."

We walked up 139th Street to Seventh Avenue

and peered through the window, but although there were sounds of the night baker in the rear, the shop was closed.

Across the avenue, the bright lights of Mickey Dee's spread like a beacon, pulling in cars and pedestrians alike, but that wasn't what I wanted. We strolled one block north to stand near the Half-Moon, where I cupped my hand against a dusty window and peered inside. The bottles and votive candles were long gone. The spindly legs of the bar stools upturned on the counter resembled the hair-like limbs of spiders lying on their backs, stiffened by time and death. I saw the quick and careful movement of rats the size of puppies making their way along the counter, gnawing probably at the glue that held the stools together.

I thought of Thea lying in the alley a few feet away with half her face gone. I closed my eyes and imagined the slow tap of Dessie's five-inch heels heading toward Lenox Avenue and the haven of Harlem Hospital.

I wondered if it had been a winter night and if she had held her coat close against the cold. Or if it had been summertime and people lounging on stoops to escape the heat of crowded apartments had waved as she passed. I wondered if the emergency room had been very crowded.

I turned away and looked up at the lamppost, where a remnant of a GRAND OPENING pennant, faded and torn, hung limply from thin wire. It was all that remained of the Half-Moon.

I walked to Eighth Avenue and headed home.

There were two messages when I returned. One was from Tad, his deep quiet voice phrasing some extraordinary ideas about my lovemaking and how hard it was for anyone to improve on a good thing. Then he calmed down enough to tell me about Roger Morris. Tad had interviewed Morris, who could offer nothing other than that he'd paid one thousand a month into Thea's bank account for her support. It turned out that he hadn't wanted a divorce after all, but hoped Thea'd change her mind and return to him when she was "ready to settle down," as he put it. Meanwhile, he had hoped and paid.

The other message was from Teddi, wanting to see me at the theater tomorrow.

I took another shower and went to bed. Sometime in the night, the phone rang, and when I answered there was silence. I pressed the call-back key but it didn't connect. I hung up and called Elizabeth Jackson, who woke up grumbling.

"Mali, I'm not going to tell you what I think of your calling me at this hour. It had better be important."

"I'm going to see Teddi tomorrow at the theater. She called while I was out. I need an update on Kendrick."

"Kendrick's okay. Teddi Big-Bucks hired another lawyer to work with me. He's a gun with heavy connections, so her boy might be seeing the light of day any day now."

"Good. I have some info on Thea that'll surprise her. I'll talk to you tomorrow afternoon. I'm meeting her at twelve."

I still couldn't sleep and spent the next hours reading the file again and trying to keep the names and dates straight. Finally I settled against the pillows, intending to think about everything. It was dawn when I opened my eyes with a bad ache in my neck and the notes scattered on the floor near the bed.

I reached for the phone and dialed Miss Adele. She came on sounding unbelievably cheerful, then got serious. "You want the clipping? What do you intend to do with it?"

"Give Teddi the information she asked for."

I hung up and showered and dressed and went uptown.

When Miss Adele opened the door, the concern showed in her face. "Are you sure you're doing the right thing?"

"I won't know until I do it, Miss Adele. There's a connection here and the longer we do nothing, the longer Kendrick looks at hard time."

She went to the cabinet, pulled out the rosewood case, and handed me the clipping. "You want me to call anyone? I don't like you stepping into something with no one to watch your back."

"I'll be fine. I'm not planning to confront anyone, just to tell Teddi what she needs to know."

Her frown grew deeper, so I said, "Okay, here are some numbers if you don't hear from me in two hours."

I gave her Bertha's number, Elizabeth's number, and the address of the theater.

"You have Dad's number, but don't call unless you really have to. He worries too much."

She jotted them down and looked at me. "Anyone else?"

I thought of Tad, but since I wasn't going to war I saw no need to call out the cavalry.

"I think that's sufficient." I pressed her hand and headed for the elevator.

"Two hours," she reminded me.

chapter twenty-seven

Star Manhattan's door was unlocked and I pushed it gently and again listened to my footfalls grow quiet and disappear as I approached the stage. Three sliding wall panels, over six feet high and painted black, were on each side with enough room to walk between each, like a narrow maze.

I quietly walked around the panels to the back. In the dressing area, the glow of a small glass-shaded lamp lit a table overflowing with the actor's usual accessories. Buried in the clutter, a small transistor with fading batteries sent out a thin crackly tune.

"Teddi?"

The name sounded cool in the silence.

"Teddi?" I called again to test the sound and also to figure who might have disappeared when they heard me step across the stage. The lamp and the radio were on. Someone had to be here. I looked around at the area, which seemed more disorganized than on my previous visit. The cables were still coiled like glutted pythons, and the trunk, empty of its contents, lay open with its lid held up by a length of iron piping. I wondered where all the stuff had gone.

I turned off the radio to allow the battery to die a decent death, then placed the chair so that my back was to the wall and sat down to wait. The silence seemed different now, and I knew I wasn't alone. I wasn't in the mood for cat and mouse, so I left the chair, approached the stage, and slipped into the maze of panels, following a faint skittering sound.

When I moved between the second and third panels, facing me at the other end was Teddi's mother, Marcella Hamilton Hamil Eden. At least I thought it was her. She came nearer, moving soundlessly on the balls of her feet, and decked out in a surprising outfit: black hooded cotton jacket, jogging pants, and black tennis shoes.

All you need, I thought, is blackface and you'd . . .

"Well, we meet again," she said. Her voice was low and her smile showed a lot more teeth than last time. The smile was by no means friendly, and I expected to hear the whine of sinister organ music break out as she approached. I did not back away because pound for pound I knew I had the advantage and could take her down without breaking a sweat. But when her hand came up out of the dark, the equation shifted: I saw the gun.

"Now," she whispered, "let's step back where we can sit and talk."

"Talk about what?" I asked. I moved back to the chair and sat down again. "I came to see Teddi. What's the problem?"

"The problem is your nosiness. Why did you come here in the first place? You weren't interested in any audition."

I considered several answers but looked at the gun again and chose the one least likely to tick her off. "Teddi called me," I said, "and here I am."

She had been standing in front of me but now eased away to sit down on a large packing crate. The gun hand never wavered.

"You're making me nervous with that weapon," I said. "Why don't you rest it?"

"I will. In my own good time. But first, let's talk."

"Fine. Where's Teddi?"

"On her way upstate to an old farmhouse where she'll be for the next week or so, working on a script. With a little luck, she should be halfway across the Tappen Zee Bridge as we speak. I left that message for you."

I said nothing. The voices had sounded so much alike on the machine. Now I wondered how long I could engage her in conversation, stall her until Miss Adele got worried. Now I was sorry I had asked her not to call Dad, but the others. What could Bert do but get more nervous? What could Elizabeth do?

"My daughter should be more careful," Marcella said. "It took some time but I managed to examine her phone bills. There were no Brooklyn numbers. Several upstate, a few Long Island, but mostly Manhattan.

Nothing even near Brooklyn. I knew Teddi was lying. At first I even thought you might be related to Kendrick—"

"That's a possibility. You know we all look alike."

She flinched as if I had struck her and I watched her brush her hair back with the same nervous gesture that Teddi used. That Thea had used. And perhaps Dessie might have also used.

I thought of the clipping in my pocket. If I died and the clipping disappeared, that would be the end of everyone's nervous condition. But it wasn't going to be that way.

"What did Teddi want?" she asked. Her voice had dropped to a whisper and an edge of impatience or panic had crept in.

Be calm, speak softly, I said to myself as I looked at her. I could manage her impatience but panic was another matter once it got out of control.

She shifted position on the edge of the packing crate and now the gun rested in her lap. Her eyes had narrowed so much I thought they had closed, but she was still on alert.

"Teddi wanted to find out more about Thea's death," I said. "And since I live in Harlem, she thought I could help her."

"And were you able to?"

"Not yet."

"Who do you think killed her?"

"Someone who's missing a diamond earring," I said, expecting to play twenty questions for at least another hour, but I miscalculated. The hand with the gun flew up and her eyes blazed wide. She moved quickly from the edge of the crate.

"You bitch! You nosy bitch! You'll be sorry you ever came down here! Get up!"

She pointed the weapon at me and waved. "Come on. Step over there. Move!"

I moved slowly, circling away from her, knowing that I couldn't move far enough, and knowing that a .45 was powerful enough to blow half my face away. Just like Thea's face.

"Stand there!"

I glanced down into the empty trunk. I was going to take the place of the junk that had been cleared out of it.

"Did you kill her?" I asked.

"You don't know?"

"No."

"Well then, you'll never know."

She maneuvered into position, never taking her eyes from me.

"How are you going to justify killing me?" I asked, stalling for more time. I had to keep her talking.

"Justify? They'll have to find you first. This trunk is going to the bottom of an old well on that farm upstate. No one interferes with my life. No one. Not Thea, not that fool in the wheelchair . . . and not you. I've worked too hard to—"

"You killed Flyin' Home?"

She didn't answer but instead lifted the gun and held it in line with my nose, steadying her aim with both hands.

I raised my arms like a traffic cop. "You think I came in here without a backup? I'm telling you: If I'm not back uptown within a few minutes, the police will be in this place in a blink."

"Well, that simply means I have to move faster, that's all."

She hesitated for the briefest second to glance at her watch in the dim light, and that was the second I needed to grab the iron pipe. The lid of the trunk slammed down and I ducked to the floor as she pulled the trigger. The recoil was terrific, and in that second I was on her with the pipe, knocking the gun from her hand. It slid across the small space and we both dove for it. She got to it first, but before she could bring it up, my hands closed on her wrist and around her throat.

"Let it go! Dammit, drop it!"

My thumb pressed on her windpipe and she flipped the gun out of her hand and kicked me in the stomach, knocking the breath out of me. I was ready to kill her now. Where was the gun? I spied it less than a foot away, and we scrambled for it. My stomach felt as if an elephant had stepped on it. She slid away from me and came up with the weapon again. She was in a crouch now, and blind with panic. Her breath was coming in deep bursts. She looked around as if I were no longer there and ran toward the maze onstage.

I backed toward the dressing table and knocked over the lamp, smashing the bulb. She had the gun. I had the darkness.

The small light still shone from center stage but was too weak to reach beyond the maze. Everything was in shadow or darkness. I bent down and crept toward the stage, freezing each time I heard movement. My eyes adjusted to the dark and I tried to gauge where the next sound might come from. I took off my shoe and threw it against the panel farthest away, and the flash and roar of the gun followed.

The acrid smell of gunpowder drifted over me as I eased along the wall toward the flash. I heard her moving away on the other side. Then she stopped. There was no movement, no breathing, no sound. Where was she? I waited, straining to hear in the dark. Then I took another step and stopped when I felt the steel nozzle pressed against the nape of my neck. She had crept so close I could feel her breath.

"Well," she said. "Thea wouldn't let sleeping dogs lie. Wouldn't stay out of my life. I got rid of her and now you come along to stir things up again." Her voice echoed in the silence. "But it's not going to happen. This is it!"

She tried to steady the weapon with both hands but still trembled violently. I looked at her face in the dim light and saw a mask of madness. There was no room for dialogue, rational or otherwise. I braced myself for what was coming but it was a different click, sharp and small—like a switch—and lights flooded the entire theater in blinding brightness.

chapter twenty-eight

Teddi leaned against the far end of the panel, wide-eyed, struggling to catch her breath. Her face was drained of color and her arms hung limply. Then she moved toward us and stopped. "Mother! What . . . what in heaven's name—?"

She moved nearer, staring past me as she held out her hands.

"Give that to me. Please, please. Don't make it any worse . . ."

I had been pressed against the panel with the weapon to my neck. When it dropped away, my heartbeat started to slow and the dryness left my throat. My tongue moved again but no words came. I began to shiver and realized that my outfit was soaked with sweat.

Marcella collapsed against the panel, and Teddi managed to get her to a chair.

"How? How?" Was all I could manage. I still couldn't speak.

Teddi shook her head slowly. "I was on my way upstate. I knew I'd be gone for a week so I called Elizabeth for a last-minute check on things. When she told me you were at the theater to meet with me, I knew something was wrong and I turned back."

I glanced at my watch and knew that Miss Adele, bless her soul, must have gotten on the drum as soon as I stepped out her door.

Teddi was leaning against the panel, studying her mother's drawn face, wondering what to say, what to do.

Finally, she whispered, "Thea wouldn't let sleeping dogs lie? Wouldn't stay out of your life? I can't believe what I just heard."

Marcella did not look at her but focused on some distant point that neither of us could see.

"She . . . she had started to blackmail me," she murmured. "Wanted to be paid for her silence—"

"No she didn't," Teddi cut in. "I saw that letter and—"

Marcella whirled to face her and I was glad Teddi had put the gun in her handbag and out of her mother's reach.

"You . . . you little sneak! You were reading my mail?"

"Not your mail, Mother. Just that particular letter that seemed to finally send you over the edge. You were always on edge, looking over your shoulder as if someone or something were shadowing you. As long as I could remember, you were running, running from one doctor to another. Pills and more pills. Neither Dad nor I could understand it.

"I couldn't figure it out until that letter. It shook you so that you dropped it and ran to your bedroom to get your pills. I don't know which ones or how many, but you were out cold in two minutes and that's when I read it."

A minute passed before Marcella found her voice. When she opened her mouth, it sounded as if she had swallowed sand. Her face was a complete blank, as if she had found one of the pills in her pocket and quickly consumed it.

"I was running. It was like running a marathon— no, like trying to stay a step ahead on a monstrous wheel. But it seems I wasn't quite fast enough."

She gazed at Teddi, then at me, and went on. "All that girl had to do was stay away. Let me live my life. That's all she had to do!"

"*That girl,* as you call her, was your daughter," Teddi said. "She was your daughter. Didn't that mean anything?"

"She was a mistake. I had no intention of allowing a mistake to ruin my life. As far as I'm concerned, she never existed."

"But why?"

"Because I didn't need any reminders about who I'd been. I was concerned with what I could become, what I did become."

Teddi eased into a chair opposite her mother and leaned forward, though she did not touch her.

"So you killed her? You killed her before I had a chance to get . . ."

"To get what?" Marcella snapped. "What did you want? Why didn't you mind your own business?"

"Thea *was* my business, Mother. Just as much as she was yours. I decided to find her. When I did, I sent her one thousand dollars a month."

Marcella sat up, leaning on the edge of her chair, her face swollen with anger. "You did what? You always *were* a fool. She would've bled you dry!"

"You're wrong. I wasn't buying her. I did it because she was my sister. And once I knew her name, it was easy to have my banker access the rest.

"I found out where she lived and I was trying to find a way to approach her, to be her friend, and then to be her sister, but I didn't move fast enough." Teddi paused, shaking her head at the wonder of it. "You got to her first. Trying to protect yourself and your stupid secret! She was black. You and I are black. I don't feel any different about myself now that I know. Why couldn't you have——?"

Marcella waved her hand. Her voice dropped low, as if she were trying to warn a child whose fingers were too near an open fan, who didn't know any better than to stick them into the blades. She spoke slowly so as not to frighten the child.

"Why couldn't I have what? It's easy enough for you to sit here and judge me. You are looking at life through the prism of wealth and privilege. Well, let me tell you: For a while I was able to do that also, but that didn't prevent me from hearing a lot of my friends——

rich, powerful, political—speak of black people in the most malicious, spiteful terms. Casual remarks privately made over private cocktails before stepping out to attend public fund-raisers for black causes. I know because I raised my glass right along with them. I heard remarks made in the presence of their own servants. As if the servants were invisible. Inhuman.

"My husband would not have married me if he had known. Your husband, a white Wall Street banker, would not have married you if he had known you had one drop of black blood, despite your blond hair and blue eyes. No. You would've ended up like your grandmother. Good enough to love but not to marry. I learned long ago that if you're black, you cannot—you *will* not be allowed to live like a human being. As far as I'm concerned, not even in this time and place. I took Thea's life to save my own. And yours."

I watched Teddi lean back with her hand to her mouth, as if her mother had exhaled a noxious germ.

"Oh, no! You didn't do it for me because I wouldn't have had a problem."

"Oh, I see. And now that you've discovered your history, I suppose you feel comfortable enough to really get involved with that jailbird?"

I saw Teddi's eyes flash, but she seemed beyond anger and the tears did not come.

"I'm not hooking up with anyone. Kendrick and I had a long talk. He loved Thea very much and that's that. And he's not the jailbird. You are. You always were. But now you get to exchange one prison cell for another. For murder."

I watched Marcella's face crumble. The errant child hadn't heard a word she'd said, so Marcella struck back hard, trying to get in a last, vicious blow. "Thea was a whore who wanted more than money," Marcella cried.

Teddi looked at her impassively. "If your daughter went that way, it's because you, and only you, sent her that way. All she wanted was for you to own up to her, to acknowledge her."

Marcella leaned back and folded her arms across her chest.

"Well, I had no intention of doing that. She was never a part of my life, so it was easier to get rid of her. I called that bar and she met me out in the alley. I had planned everything. I even drove by there several times and I knew exactly what I was going to do.

"I wore the same clothes I'm wearing now and I carried the same gun—your father's gun."

She drew a breath and went on, sounding proud of what she had accomplished. I could not believe that anyone could be so blind, so filled with self-loathing.

"This hooded jacket," Marcella continued, "glasses, dark makeup and in the confusion, I walked away from that alley to my car. I didn't even run. I walked. There was that cripple in his wheelchair. He slipped away but not for long. I knew I'd find him."

She turned to me then with a look that could keep a body frozen for years. "I saw you with him. You also got away once, but I knew I would see you again."

"Marcella, you killed a man for nothing," I said. "He didn't see you well enough to identify you. You killed him for nothing. Just like you killed your daughter. Now here you are, facing some serious hard time."

Marcella closed her eyes and brushed her hair from her face. Her careful makeup could not conceal the shock of revelation, and age seemed to creep through even as I watched her.

"You don't understand. I have always faced hard time. And since it no longer matters, yes, that was my earring. Sometime later, I misplaced the other one and I can't remember where . . . like the other part of my life, I can't remember."

She began to cry, but Teddi, leaning back in her chair, did not move. She simply watched.

I turned and walked up the aisle. There was a phone downstairs in the lobby and I dialed Tad's number.

When I returned, Marcella was slouched in her chair and her face had again taken on a blank expression. Teddi was crying now and I wondered if her tears were for Thea's lost life or for her mother's.

I sat down next to Teddi to listen for the faint siren of the police, and I thought of Dessie, who, out of love, had struggled to do the right thing.

"Listen, Teddi," I said. "There's a beautiful picture of your grandmother I think you might like to have."

"My grandmother?" She turned to look at me. "Of course I'm interested. Where is it?"

"Senator Michaels—*ex*-Senator Michaels—has it. Have your attorney contact him. Mention Thea's bankbook and Michaels'll have that picture in your hand in a matter of days. Right now, he can't handle any more scandal, so it shouldn't be a problem. I'll be glad to help you because Miss Adele wants a copy also."

She nodded her head, as if coming out of a deep sleep. Her tears had dried and she seemed more composed.

"Is Miss Adele a relative also?"

"You might say that," I murmured. "She can tell you everything you need to know. And she also serves the coldest champagne I ever tasted."

chapter twenty-nine

hen the American Airlines jet touched down and Alvin rushed through the crowd toward us, I almost didn't recognize him. He looked taller, older, and more muscular. I watched his loping stride and wondered where his childhood had gone. It had been here just two months ago.

"Hi Mali! Grandpa! Kendrick, man, how you doin'?" He hugged us and stepped back to look at Kendrick. "Yo, man. Even your bumps got muscles. You musta been into some serious weights."

Kendrick shrugged as we made our way to the baggage area, where Alvin scooped up his duffel. In the parking lot, we piled into Kendrick's car and headed toward the Long Island Expressway. The charges against Kendrick had been dismissed when Marcella was arrested, but he wanted to tell Alvin the story himself. It wouldn't sound right, he said, coming from anyone else.

But Alvin was still excited about his vacation and we let him talk. "Do you know that a Captain Bill Pinckney from Chicago and Captain Ted Seymour from the Virgin Islands are the only two black men to have sailed around the world solo? Seymour did it in 1987 and Pinckney did it in 1992 in a forty-seven-foot yacht."

I was impressed. We were all impressed.

"Guess what I'm going to do when I finish college, Grandpa?"

Dad smiled. "You're going to sail solo around the world. Why not?"

I said nothing. College was at least six more years away. Time enough for me to come to terms with my nervousness and with whatever he wanted to do with his life.

"So Kendrick, what's been happening? What'd I miss?"

I sat back and watched the landscape of Queens flit by as Kendrick maneuvered through the traffic. He recounted the events in a straightforward way, and by the time we'd crossed the Triboro Bridge and had eased through a break to turn toward the Harlem River Drive, the story was over.

For several minutes, Alvin gazed out of the window. Then he looked at Dad, and at Kendrick, and turned to glance back at me. "I didn't know love could be so much trouble."

There was a short silence before Dad replied. "Depends, my boy. It all depends."

"On what?" Alvin asked. His young face was clouded with concern.

When no one answered, he shook his head. "Well, all I can say is: That solo trip 'round the world is lookin' better and better."

This time we really had no answer, but Kendrick managed to smile as he lowered the window. The noise of traffic rushed in as we came off the drive at 135th Street and headed home.

"Wait and see, Alvin. Wait and see," he smiled.

about the author

GRACE F. EDWARDS was born and raised in Harlem and currently lives in Brooklyn. Her first novel, *In the Shadow of the Peacock,* was published in 1988. Her first mystery, *If I Should Die,* debuted in May 1997.

If you enjoyed Grace Edwards' A TOAST BEFORE DYING, you will not want to miss any of the mysteries in this critically acclaimed series.

You'll find the next mystery featuring Mali Anderson, NO TIME TO DIE, coming in hardcover from Doubleday Books in Summer 1999, at your favorite bookseller. Don't miss it!